Inside the kitchen, using a paper towel to wipe squashed banana off Tyler's forehead, was a young woman I'd never seen before.

Her hair was short and spiky and dyed purple. She had lots and lots of earrings, plus one small gold hoop through her eyebrow and another through her nostril. She wore silver rings on her thumbs, middle fingers and pinkies. Creeping down from under the sleeves of her tight black T-shirt were tattoos: A red rose on a thorny stem on her left arm, and an intricate black design on her right.

The strange woman straightened up. She and I stared at each other.

"Who are you?" I asked.

"Heavenly Litebody," she answered.

I waited for her to ask who I was, but she didn't. Instead she turned back to Tyler and continued to wipe banana off his face.

"What are you doing here?" I asked.

"I work here," she said without looking up.

"Since when?" I asked.

Here Comes Heavenly #1
Here Comes Heavenly #2: Dance Magic

AGAINST THE ODDS™: Shark Bite
AGAINST THE ODDS™: Grizzly Attack
AGAINST THE ODDS™: Buzzard's Feast
AGAINST THE ODDS™: Gator Prey

HERE COMES HEAVENLY

Todd Strasser

SIMON PULSE
New York London Toronto Sydney Singapore

First Simon Pulse edition August 2002
Text copyright © 1999 by Todd Strasser
First Archway Paperback printing October 1999

SIMON PULSE
An imprint of Simon & Schuster
Children's Publishing Division
1230 Avenue of the Americas
New York, NY 10020

Printed in USA

10 9 8 7 6 5

ISBN 0-671-03626-2

to the helpful and friendly staff
of the Larchmont Public Library

Chapter

1

I will never forget the first time I saw Heavenly Litebody. It was the morning after our last nanny packed her bags and walked out of the house without saying good-bye. Mom and Dad were away on business trips as usual. I came downstairs hoping there'd be some milk and cold cereal for breakfast. Or maybe, if I was really lucky, some bread for toast.

I don't want you to think that we were poor or anything like that. Actually (we were never supposed to say this), I think we were sort of rich. We lived in a big, old house that Mom and Dad had spent a fortune fixing up. My parents both had very important jobs that required them to be away almost all the time. Once a year—when they could both take a week off at the same time—our whole family and the nanny would fly to some incredible resort where Mom and Dad would rent three rooms for the children (one for the girls, one for the boys, and one for the nanny and the baby) and a suite for themselves.

Anyway, the reason there wasn't much food in the house was because our last nanny insisted that buying food for us wasn't part of her job. As far as she was concerned, she was supposed to take care of the baby and no one else. The only laundry she did was the baby's, and the only food she bought was for him (and herself, of course). Mom and Dad weren't happy about that. They said they were going to fire her and get a new nanny as soon as they had the time, but they never did. Instead, they usually left us money to eat out and to take our clothes to the laundry.

But on the morning I'm talking about it was cold, windy and rainy outside. I really didn't want to go out for breakfast in weather like that, especially since I'd gotten up early to put on make-up, fix my hair extra nice and pick out a wicked sharp outfit. I needed to look my best because that was the day I absolutely *had* to make sure I got Roy Chandler for my history project partner.

As I went downstairs, the first thing I noticed were the aromas in the air. It smelled as if someone was *cooking!* And I don't mean popping popcorn in the microwave or heating Pop Tarts in the toaster. It smelled like bacon and eggs and pancakes. Like what you'd find in a cozy little diner or a country inn.

This was definitely strange. It couldn't be the nanny who was cooking because even if she'd had a change of heart and come back, why would she make breakfast? And where had the food come from? I doubted it was Mom home early from her most recent business trip because, to tell you the truth, she never cooked much even when she was home.

So who could it be?

Even stranger was the voice I heard coming from the kitchen: "Okay, Tyler, you little wiggler, here's your bacon and eggs. And your banana cut up just the way you like it. And your orange juice. Now what do you say?"

"This is my nose," I heard Tyler answer. We called Tyler the baby even though he was two years old.

"No kidding, kid," said the stranger. "But what do you say?"

"This is my eye."

"Right again, but check this: When someone makes you a nice yummy breakfast in the morning, you're supposed to say something. Do you know what it is?"

"This is my toes."

"No, sweetie. It's *'these are* my toes.' Now,

back to the main event. When someone makes you a nice yummy breakfast in the morning, you're supposed to say, 'Thank you.'"

"This is banana."

"Right, Mr. Messy Face, that's banana, and it goes in your mouth, not on your forehead."

I'd stopped outside the kitchen to listen to all of this. I couldn't begin to imagine who it could be. Not only did our last nanny refuse to cook, she hardly ever *spoke*, except to grumble and mutter things we couldn't understand.

Yet, try as hard as I could, I couldn't figure out who was in our kitchen. We just didn't know anybody who sounded like that.

I couldn't stand the suspense any longer. I pushed on the kitchen door and went in.

Chapter

Inside the kitchen, using a paper towel to wipe squashed banana off Tyler's forehead, was a young woman I'd never seen before. She wasn't young the way I was young, which is to say, 14 at the time. But she was young the way a student teacher at school might be young.

Only you never saw a student teacher who looked like this. Her hair was short and spiky and dyed purple. She had lots and lots of earrings, plus one small gold hoop through her eyebrow and another through her nostril. She wore silver rings on her thumbs, middle fingers and pinkies. Creeping down from under the sleeves of her tight black T-shirt were tattoos: A red rose on a thorny stem on her left arm, and an intricate black design on her right arm.

"Kitty Kat, Kitty Kat!" screeched Tyler, sitting

5

in his highchair with his face smeared with eggs and banana. My real name is Caitlin Rand, but everyone calls me Kit. Except Tyler, who calls me Kitty Kat.

The strange woman straightened up. She and I stared at each other.

"Who are you?" I asked.

"Heavenly Litebody," she answered.

I waited for her to ask who I was, but she didn't. Instead she turned back to Tyler and continued to wipe banana off his face.

"What are you doing here?" I asked.

"I work here," she said without looking up.

"Since when?" I asked. After all, our last nanny had only quit the night before. Mom and Dad were still away. We hadn't even told them yet.

Heavenly Litebody didn't answer my question. Instead, she crumpled up the napkin she'd used to wipe breakfast off Tyler's face and tossed it onto the kitchen counter.

"Remember, Tyler Tot," she said, "when someone gives you a yummy breakfast, you're supposed to say thank you."

"Thank you," said Tyler. "Thank you, thank you, thank you, thank you, thank you, thank—"

"Once is enough, buster." Heavenly Litebody moved over to the stove and started to stir a batch of scrambled eggs in a pan.

"Uh, excuse me, but how did you even get into our house?" I asked. The night before, after the last nanny stormed out and left us all alone, I went through the entire house making sure all the doors and windows were locked. Then Robby set the alarm system. It was supposed to be the best security system money could buy. Dad called it "state of the art" although what it had to do with art was a mystery to me.

"I let myself in," Heavenly Litebody answered as she slid clumps of steaming scrambled eggs onto five plates. I could feel my stomach begin to grumble hungrily.

"But you don't know the code."

"T, R, S, K, C," replied Heavenly.

I felt my mouth fall open. That was our family's secret code! It was based on the first letters of each kid's name: Tyler, Samara, Robby, Kit and Chance. But no one, absolutely *no one*, was supposed to know!

"Who told you?" I sputtered.

Tyler picked up a glob of scrambled egg and made a fist. Thin slabs of yellow squeezed out between his pudgy little fingers and fell to the floor.

"That's all the breakfast you're going to get, Mr. Make-a-Mess." Heavenly took Tyler's plate from the highchair.

"No!" Tyler cried and reached out with his

egg-streaked hands. "Gimme gimme more more."

But Heavenly was already scraping the remaining eggs and bacon off his plate and into the garbage. "Sorry, pal, but no one plays with food in my kitchen."

"*Your* kitchen?" I asked, totally confused.

"Gimme more!" Tyler screeched and started to kick and cry in the highchair. Our past nannies had always hurried to pick him up and cuddle him when he threw a tantrum. Heavenly ignored him. She handed me a plate with bacon and steaming scrambled eggs. "White, whole wheat or rye toast?"

Tyler was still kicking and screaming in his highchair. His face had turned red. I stared down at the plate of food and then up at Heavenly. "Really, who are you?"

"I told you," she said as she turned back to the oven. "My name is Heavenly Litebody and I work here. And frankly, that's all you need to know. Now you better eat breakfast and get ready for school or you're going to be late."

Tyler was still screaming and red-faced and thrashing around so hard that his highchair had begun to buck across the kitchen floor.

And that's when Chance arrived.

Chapter

*C*hance was Dad's son and my stepbrother. At 16, he was tall and wiry with brown hair that fell into his dark eyes. All the girls at school were jealous of me because he was movie-star gorgeous, but also athletic and funny. The problem was that they didn't have to *live* with him.

"Whoa! What is *this?*" Chance asked with a grin as he swept his hair out of his eyes. He was bare-chested and his jeans hung low on his hips, revealing the tops of his blue plaid boxer shorts.

"It's called breakfast," Heavenly informed him from the stove, "but not until you put on a shirt."

Chance kept grinning. That's just the way he was—the sort of guy who treated everything as a joke and never seemed to take anything seriously.

"Who're you?" he asked.

"Her name's Heavenly Litebody and she says she works here," I said. "I have no idea who hired her or how she got our alarm code."

"Whaaaaaaaaaa!" Tyler let out a particularly loud wail. I guess he felt ignored.

"Chill out, little dude, you're killing my eardrums." Chance started toward Tyler, as if he was going to pick him up. Heavenly waved a spatula at him in a slightly menacing way.

"I'd appreciate it if you stayed out of this," she said.

"What?" Chance asked with a look of surprise.

"She's teaching him a lesson," I explained.

"Twisted." Chance chuckled. "If there's one thing this family needs, it's lessons."

He was joking, of course. Chance *hated* lessons.

Heavenly wasn't amused. "So where's that shirt, stud?"

Chance ignored her. He crossed the kitchen and opened the refrigerator. His normal breakfast consisted of a can of Snapple or a Coke. If he was really hungry, he'd throw in a few chocolate chip cookies.

He pulled out a can of Mountain Dew. But as he closed the refrigerator, he found himself face to face with Heavenly.

"That's not for breakfast," she said.

"Say what?" Chance made a face.

"Put it back in the refrigerator, put on a shirt, and have a decent meal," Heavenly ordered.

If there was one thing Chance hated even more than lessons, it was orders. The jaunty smile vanished. He narrowed his eyes.

"Look, I don't know what punk weirdo cave you crawled out of, but do me a favor and get stuffed." Chance was serious. He started to go around Heavenly, but she blocked his path and held up the spatula.

"Do as I say," she said calmly but firmly.

The lines in my stepbrother's forehead deepened. "Listen, uh, whatever your name is, I don't know you, you don't work here, and I don't have to listen to you."

Once again, he started to go around her.

And that's when things got really strange.

Chapter

As Chance stepped around Heavenly, he slipped his finger into the tab of the soda can and pulled. But instead of opening, the tab broke off.

"Oh, man," Chance muttered. He turned back to the refrigerator and took out another can. He put his finger in the tab and pulled. Once again, the tab broke off before the can opened.

Now, everyone knows that once in a while the tab breaks off a can of soda. But when was the last time you saw it happen twice in a row?

With a major scowl on his face, Chance took yet another can from the refrigerator. This time he very carefully slid his finger into the tab and very, very carefully pulled.

With a tiny *clink!* the tab broke off.

Three times in a row?

The kitchen was silent. Even Tyler, who was too young to understand how strange this was, had stopped bawling, probably because he sensed something truly weird was going on.

"What are the chances of *that* happening?" Chance asked and went over to the kitchen counter. He pulled open one drawer, then another, and then a third. "Where's the can opener?"

"Put the cans back, put on a shirt, and come for breakfast," Heavenly said calmly.

Chance forced a smile onto his face. Only this smile seemed ominous and unfriendly. "Not if my life depended on it." He slammed the last can of soda down on the kitchen counter, then stormed out.

Heavenly put the cans back into the refrigerator. Then she turned to Tyler.

"Want to get out of the highchair, Mr. Wiggler?" she asked.

Tyler nodded and held out his arms the way he did when he wanted one of us to take him. Usually he wouldn't let a nanny do that if Chance, Robby or I were around. He always wanted us to do it.

But he let Heavenly lift him out of the chair and put him on the floor. Then he waddled off toward the den.

I don't think I'd moved since Chance took

the first can of soda out of the refrigerator.
Heavenly went back to the kitchen counter and
started buttering toast as if nothing had happened.

"Do you know if your brother and sister are
up?" she asked.

"Uh, no," I answered. Another grumble from
my stomach reminded me that I was hungry.
Heavenly brought over my toast. Breakfast
smelled so good. I speared a forkful of eggs and
ate it.

"This is good," I said.

"Thank you," Heavenly replied.

I took another bite and another. I have a ten-
dency to eat fast. I know it's a bad habit, but it's
hard to break, especially when I'm eating something that tastes good. I know it must seem
weird, I mean, eating this breakfast made by
this total stranger who somehow appeared in
our kitchen without any explanation. But if
you knew how many nannies we'd gone
through since Tyler was born—six in two years,
I think—then you'd understand that for us it
wasn't so unusual.

Except . . .

"How do you know I have another brother
and sister?" I asked as I dabbed my lips with my
napkin.

"T, R, S, K, C," Heavenly replied.

"Yes, but—"

"If you're finished," Heavenly went on, "go upstairs and make sure they're up. I don't want them to be late for school."

I got up and started out of the kitchen.

"Kit?" Heavenly's voice stopped me.

"Yes?"

She nodded back at the kitchen table. "Your dirty dishes."

"Huh?"

"We don't leave them on the kitchen table, do we?"

"Oh . . . I guess not." I went back and brought my dishes to the sink, then headed upstairs. I had to find Chance, and figure out what we should do.

Chapter

5

I don't care," Chance said as he buttoned his shirt. I was in his room. Chance was a collector of strange things and his room was cluttered with all kinds of junk. In one corner was a wheel from a motorcycle. Against the wall was a surfboard with a big chunk missing. On his desk was a bent propeller from an outboard engine. The walls were covered with torn out magazine ads for snowboards and surfboards and mountain bikes. On his bed were stacks of CDs, books and magazines. Chance never slept in his bed. He preferred a thin mattress on the floor.

"You *have* to care," I insisted. "Mom and Dad are away. This Heavenly person is a stranger. I mean, how can we leave her alone in the house with Tyler while we all go to school? What if she's a kidnapper or something?"

Chance gave me one of his "get real" looks.

"I'm serious," I said.

"Then you stay home with Tyler," Chance said.

"I can't," I said.

"Why not?"

I felt my face turn red. "Because."

Chance gave me a curious look. "Because what?"

"None of your business."

"Does it have something to do with why you've fixed up your hair, put on make-up and decided to wear a short skirt?" he asked with a sly grin.

My face felt even hotter. Why did Chance have to be so perceptive?

"I thought so." He nodded knowingly.

"It's no big deal," I tried to explain. "We're just picking partners for a history project."

"And there's someone special you want as your partner," Chance guessed.

"Maybe."

"Some cute guy, huh?"

"Can we get back to the subject?" I said. "Why can't *you* stay home?"

"I don't want to."

"Why not?" I asked. "You cut school once a week anyway. At least this time you'd have a good excuse."

"Forget it."

I got the feeling that staying home with the mysterious and bossy Heavenly was the last thing Chance wanted to do.

"Chance, seriously, I don't feel right about this."

"About what?" It was my ten-year-old brother Robby, standing in the doorway in his green Kermit the Frog pajamas. Robby had short brown hair and was sort of chubby.

"Nothing, Robby," I said.

"Go ahead and tell him," Chance said. "He'll find out as soon as he goes downstairs anyway."

"Find out what?" Robby asked.

"There's some weirdo downstairs," Chance said.

"Weirdo?" Robby repeated with a scowl.

"She says she works here and she's kind of acting like Tyler's nanny," I explained. "She even cooked us breakfast. But I don't know who she is or where she came from."

"Did she say what her name was?" Robby asked.

"Heavenly Litebody," I said. "Can you believe it?"

To my total surprise, Robby nodded, and turned as white as vanilla ice cream.

Chapter

6

W hat's with you?" I asked.

"Well, uh, I think I know where she came from. Come on, I'll show you." Robby spun around and headed for his room. Chance and I followed.

Robby's room was typical of most ten-year-old boys'. His walls were covered with posters of professional wrestlers and racing cars. His shelves were filled with books he'd never read, Lego models and little sports trophies (he wasn't much of an athlete, but at his age you got a trophy in a sport just for showing up). Also, like most kids his age, the centerpiece of his room was his computer.

Robby sat down and began to type. I heard the faint blips of a phone number being dialed and then the blurps and bleeps of a modem connecting.

"Mind telling us what this is about?" Chance asked.

"Last night," Robby said as he hit more keys, "after the nanny quit I went online to find a new one."

"You can find nannies on the Internet?" I asked.

"Why not?" Robby replied. "You can find everything else. The big problem is most live too far away and I figured we needed one fast . . . gee, where is it?"

"Where's what?" Chance asked behind him.

"InstantNanny.com," Robby said.

"What is InstantNanny.com?" I asked.

"This really cool website. I don't get it. It was here last night. I even bookmarked it."

Robby pointed at the words INSTANTNANNY.COM on the screen.

But the computer was showing the message WEBSITE NOT FOUND.

"It's not possible." Robby typed feverishly. "Websites don't disappear overnight."

"Forget about the website," Chance said. "Just tell us what happened."

"I went there," Robby said, refusing to give up the search.

"Went where?" I asked.

"InstantNanny.com," Robby said. "And they

had all these pages with different nannies on them . . . and all the nannies had these weird names."

"Like Heavenly Litebody?" I guessed.

"Sort of," Robby said. "This is totally weird . . . the logo's in the cache but the website's gone."

"Forget about the website," Chance said again.

"How did she get here?" I asked.

"I don't know," Robby said. "All I did was leave a message."

"What message?" Chance asked.

"That we had an emergency," Robby said. "Our nanny quit and our parents were away. We all had to go to school today and there was no one to watch Tyler. So they should send someone ASAP."

I looked at Chance. "You think it's possible that she came from the Internet?"

My stepbrother raised his hands and shrugged. "Hey, she's here, isn't she?"

But something else was bothering me. "Did you let her in this morning?" I asked Robby.

Robby shook his head.

"Tell the truth, Robby," I said. "Either someone let her in the house or you gave her the alarm code."

Robby widened his eyes and shook his head. "I didn't! I swear! I'd never do that! I didn't even know about her until I heard you two talking in Chance's room."

21

Chance and I shared another look. Whenever he fixed me with those dark eyes, I felt a shiver run down my skin. He was so gorgeous. Maybe the girls at school were right to feel jealous.

I turned back to Robby. "Did that website say anything about where she came from?"

"I don't remember," Robby answered.

"I still don't understand how she got past the alarm system," I said to Robby. "You're *sure* you didn't tell her?"

"I swear!" Robby cried.

I believed him. Robby was still young enough to think that if you told a lie someone really powerful like God or Bill Gates would send a virus into your computer that would eat up all your favorite games.

Chance swept the hair out of his eyes. "Well, folks, that leaves only one other possible suspect."

Chapter

Just in case you've gotten confused, let me take a moment to explain our family setup. This was the second marriage for both Mom and Dad (my stepdad). Robby and I were Mom's kids. Chance was Dad's son. And Tyler was the product of both of them. But Dad also brought a daughter to the marriage. Her name was Samara and she was twelve and the rest of us hated her.

Chance, Robby and I stopped outside Samara's bedroom. On her door was a neatly printed sign that said:

THIS DOOR IS LOCKED.

PLEASE KNOCK AND WAIT.

DO NOT TOUCH THE DOORKNOB.

THANK YOU.

We could hear music coming from inside. Samara was singing along to it in her screechy voice. Not as bad as fingernails scraping against a blackboard. But close.

Chance knocked. "Samara?"

"Who is it?" a voice called from inside.

"Darth Vader."

"Just a minute."

The three of us stood outside her door and waited. Samara loved to make you wait. I noticed a bright-red ladybug crawling up the wall next to Samara's door, and wondered how it had gotten into the house.

"What's Samara doing?" Robby asked impatiently.

"Preparing to meet her subjects," I said.

"What?" Robby didn't understand.

"Nothing." I looked back at the ladybug, but it was gone. Meanwhile, we could hear Samara still singing along with the music.

Chance knocked again.

"I said, just a minute!" Samara called from inside.

"You better open up," Chance warned. "Or I just might hawk up a big gob and leave it on your doorknob."

Inside, Samara ignored him and kept singing.

"Sheesh!" Chance grabbed the doorknob and tried to turn it, but it was locked.

Within seconds the door swung open. Samara

was wearing a neatly pressed blouse and skirt. Her light brown hair was very precisely brushed and held back with a barrette. She was wearing the faintest makeup. She glowered at Chance and pointed to the sign on her door.

"Can't you read?" she huffed.

"Nope," Chance answered.

Samara let out a big, dramatic sigh and went back into her room. She returned a moment later with a paper towel and a can of disinfectant which she sprayed on the doorknob.

"Did anyone ever tell you you're totally demented?" Chance asked.

Samara wiped the doorknob clean and tossed the paper towel into her wastepaper basket. "How did I ever wind up with someone as crude as you for a brother?"

"How did I ever wind up with someone as weird as you for a sister?" Chance shot back.

"What do you want?" Samara asked impatiently, looking at all of us.

"What do you know about Heavenly Litebody?" I asked.

Samara scowled and touched her hair self-consciously. "Is it a new shampoo?"

"No, it's a new nanny," Chance said.

"Who?" Samara asked.

"The person you let into the house this morning," I said.

"I don't know what you're talking about," Samara said.

"Then how did she get in?" I asked.

Just then the intercom crackled on. I guess I better explain why we had an intercom. It's because our house had three stories. Four, if you include the basement. They're not allowed to build three-story houses anymore because of the fire code. But our house was really old (though completely modernized). So in order to save people from screaming themselves hoarse when they needed someone two floors away, my parents had an intercom installed.

"Anyone who hasn't had breakfast better come right now," Heavenly called from down-stairs. "The kitchen closes in ten minutes!"

"The kitchen closes?" Samara repeated with a perplexed look.

"What's for breakfast?" asked Robby, who loved eating almost as much as computer games.

"Bacon, eggs and toast," I said.

"See ya!" Robby hurried downstairs.

"You *sure* you don't know how she got here?" I asked Samara one last time.

My stepsister shook her head.

"Listen, Kit," Chance said. "I don't think the question is how she *got* here. I think the question is, how are we going to *get rid* of her?"

Chapter

w, come on, that's no fair!" we heard Robby wail as we went back downstairs.

In the kitchen, Robby was sitting at the table eating breakfast. Heavenly was standing at the kitchen counter. Spread out on the counter was a loaf of bread, a jar of peanut butter, some sliced meats and cheeses, some apples and bananas, and four white paper bags.

It appeared that Heavenly was making us lunch.

Robby gave us a pained look. "Will you tell her that granola bars are good for you? She says they're candy and she'll only let me take one for the whole day."

Chance smirked. "Gee, Robby, just *one* granola bar and lunch for the whole day? You'll probably starve to death."

Robby nodded and pointed at Heavenly. "That's what I told her."

"A chocolate-covered caramel granola bar is nothing but fat and sugar," Heavenly informed him. "And stop pointing, it's not polite."

Robby stopped pointing, but kept pouting. Meanwhile, Heavenly turned to Chance.

"I see you changed your mind and put on a shirt," she said. "Would you like some breakfast now?"

Chance gazed hungrily at the bacon and eggs and toast. It had been a long time since anyone had made us a hot breakfast, and I had a feeling he was really tempted to eat it. But he shook his head.

Heavenly tossed her head as if she didn't care. "Suit yourself. Just make your bed before you go to school."

Those of us in the kitchen shared astonished glances. *Make our beds?*

Samara crossed her arms. "I already did."

"Good for you," Heavenly said, handing her a plate of eggs, bacon and toast. "Have your breakfast."

Samara stared down her nose at the plate. "Sorry, I don't eat breakfast. I can't even *think* about food until lunch."

Heavenly leveled her gaze at her. "Breakfast is the most important meal of the day."

"Not my day," replied Samara.

Meanwhile, Chance quietly left the kitchen and started for the front door. I think he hoped to sneak out unnoticed.

"Your bed and lunch, Mister!" Heavenly called after him.

Out in the front hall, Chance didn't answer. Heavenly turned her attention back to Samara. "I made this breakfast for you."

"No one told you to," Samara shot back. "What are you doing here anyway? Where did you come from?"

"She's not going to tell you," I said.

Chance reappeared in the doorway with a sour expression on his face. He held up a brass doorknob. It had come from the front door.

"You didn't make your bed," Heavenly said.

"I never sleep in my bed," Chance said.

"Then you straighten up wherever you do sleep," Heavenly replied.

Except for Samara, we never made our beds. On the days when Fortuna, our cleaning lady came, she made them.

"What's the point of making our beds when we're just going to sleep in them again tonight?" I asked.

"A man who sits on a tack gets the point," said Robby, who just loved dumb jokes.

"The point," Heavenly replied, "is that we're civilized human beings, not a bunch of squirrels nesting in trees. We eat the right things for breakfast, and we make our beds because that's what we're supposed to do."

"Are we supposed to dye our hair purple and pierce our eyebrows?" Chance asked.

"What's that got to do with anything?" Heavenly shot back.

No one answered. After a moment, Chance held up the doorknob. "What are we going to do about this?"

Heavenly took the doorknob out of his hand. "I'll take care of it while you straighten upstairs."

Chance stared at her for a moment, then headed upstairs. Robby and I shared a funny look and then followed him. As we left the kitchen, we could hear Heavenly once again telling Samara to eat her breakfast.

Back upstairs, I made my bed. A ladybug was crawling up my bedpost. I wondered if it was the same one I saw outside Samara's room. I could hear Chance in his room, muttering to himself. A few moments later I came out into the hallway. Chance and Robby were already there. Robby had his backpack full of books. Chance never brought books home from school.

My stepbrother's hands were jammed into his pants pockets and his lips were pursed with anger. "What's the record for the shortest time a nanny has ever stayed with us?" he asked in a low voice.

"Remember that one from Iowa?" Robby asked. "I think she only stayed a week."

"Well," Chance said, "this one's gonna stay even less."

Chapter

When we got back downstairs, Heavenly was putting Tyler into the stroller. Of all the weird things that had happened that morning, this had to be one of the weirdest. Tyler hated getting into the stroller. He usually spent the mornings in front of the television—and the afternoons and evenings, too. I couldn't imagine how Heavenly had convinced him.

"Where are you going?" I asked, still worried that she might kidnap him.

"Just out for some fresh air," Heavenly replied.

"Our nanny usually drives us to school in the morning," Robby said as he took his jacket out of the front closet.

"Does she?" Heavenly raised an eyebrow.

"Aren't we driving?" Samara asked behind us.

"Doesn't look like it," I answered.

"But it's raining!" she complained. "My shoes will get wet!"

"Tsk, tsk, such a hard life," Heavenly teased sarcastically.

"It's cold and wet out," I said. It wasn't that school was far away; we just never walked.

"Yeah," Chance said with a joking grin. "You don't want Kit to miss the opportunity to get the boy of her dreams, do you?"

"Get stuffed!" I snapped at him.

"Walking is good for you," Heavenly replied. She pulled a big bulky brown sweater on over her head. It fit her like a sack. Then she wrapped a bright red scarf around her neck.

"Forget this, I'm calling Jared," Chance said. Jared was his friend, whose mother always drove him to school. Chance went into the kitchen. Heavenly started to snap a clear plastic rain cover over Tyler's stroller.

A few moments later, Chance was back.

"Can I get a ride, too?" Samara asked.

"No one's getting a ride." Chance scratched his head. "Jared's line was busy. So were all my other friends'."

"Maybe they were on the phone," Robby said.

"They all have call waiting," Chance said.

Out of the corner of my eye, I thought I saw a small smile on Heavenly's face.

Having no choice but to walk, we all gathered at the front door. It was easier to leave together in the morning because it was a pain to deactivate and then reset the alarm.

Standing near Heavenly, I thought I smelled the most unusual scent. It was sort of sweet and sour. Raspberry and lemon.

"Everyone ready?" Robby asked and deactivated the alarm. He pulled open the door and a gust of cold, wet air washed over us. Everyone went out the door and then waited outside while Robby reset the alarm. Our breaths came out in white plumes of vapor. Rainwater dripped from the eaves of the house.

"Later, geeks." Chance spotted some of his friends down the street. He took off in a jog to catch up to them. The rest of us started to walk down the sidewalk. Heavenly pushed Tyler in the stroller.

Most of the houses in our neighborhood are big and more than 100 years old. But they've all been fixed up with fresh paint and new roofs and neatly trimmed lawns.

As we walked up Soundview Avenue toward school, we crossed several streets. Most were normal size, but one was twice as wide as the others.

"Here's a riddle," Robby said. "What did Tennessee?"

Heavenly rolled her eyes as if it was obvious. "Everyone knows the answer is 'What Arkansas.'"

"No fair!" Robby complained. "Okay, here's something you'll never know the answer to. I bet you don't know why Cedar Street is twice as wide as all the others."

"Maybe because the old trolley line used to end here," Heavenly said. "They built Cedar Street extra wide because they needed room to turn the trolleys around and send them back into town."

Robby's mouth fell open. "How'd you know that?"

"You think you know everything?" Heavenly asked in a teasing way.

"No, but you'd have to come from right around here to know that," Robby said.

"Maybe I do." Heavenly winked.

It was almost time for the school doors to open. Cars driven by mothers and nannies passed us as we walked along the sidewalk. A girl with long blond hair passed in a car. It was Jessica Havretal Huffington, my arch enemy in the war over who would get Roy Chandler as a partner for our history project. I could feel my stomach start to knot. It had to be me. It just *had* to!

"Oh, gee!" Robby suddenly said, bringing me out of my thoughts. He looked at Heavenly. "How're you going to get back into the house?"

"I'll let myself back in," Heavenly informed him.

"You can't," Robby said. "You don't have a key and you don't know how to work the alarm."

"I *do* have a key and I *do* know how to work the alarm," Heavenly replied. "I don't know why you bother to have that dumb alarm, though. What you folks need is a large dog."

For the first time I found something likable about her. "You really think so?" I asked hopefully. "I would do anything for a dog!"

"No way!" Samara cried.

"What's your problem?" Heavenly asked.

"She's afraid of them," Robby said.

"I am not!" Samara insisted. "But they drool and shed and track dirt all over the house. Mom says there's no way she'd ever let us get one. And Dad says he doesn't want the responsibility."

"Having a dog isn't a responsibility," Heavenly corrected her. "It's a pleasure. Dogs are much smarter than we are."

"How can you say that?" Samara asked. "They go around sniffing each other."

Robby giggled.

"That's the way they communicate," Heavenly

said. "We'd probably be a lot better off if we went around sniffing each other too."

"That's so gross!" Samara cried.

I had to smile, but Samara stared at Heavenly like she was crazy.

"Anyway, it would never work," Samara concluded. "Puff would hate him."

Puff was our cat.

"That's not necessarily true," Heavenly replied. "And a dog will always love you. He'll always forgive you no matter what you've done. And he'll always be your friend."

"Which side of a dog has more hair?" Robby asked.

"The outside," answered Heavenly.

"Rats!" Robby clenched his fists and fumed.

Robby went to the elementary school. Samara and I went to the middle school and Chance was in high school. All the schools were bunched together on the same "campus." They were just in different buildings.

When we got to the elementary school, kids were being dropped off by mothers and nannies in big shiny cars. A lot of the mothers were thin and blond and dressed in fancy clothes. Even some of the nannies were thin and blond and dressed in fancy clothes.

As we got close, people's heads began to turn. I saw funny expressions on some of their faces. Others stared openly at Heavenly's dyed hair and the gold hoops in her nose and eye-brow.

Feeling self-conscious, Robby, Samara and I began to slow down. Heavenly didn't notice and pushed the stroller ahead. She only noticed when we were all about a dozen feet behind her.

"Come on; you don't want to be late, do you?" she said.

We shook our heads, but we were in no rush to catch up, either.

"You don't have to walk us the rest of the way," Samara said. "We can get to school by ourselves."

Heavenly scowled. Then she looked around as if she was suddenly aware of the mothers and other nannies. She turned back to us with a surprised look on her face. The three of us had stopped on the sidewalk.

"What is this?" Heavenly asked loudly enough for everyone to hear. "You're ashamed to be seen with me?"

The three of us stood there, slack-jawed and not knowing what to say.

"You're embarrassed because I'm not blond with skinny legs and diamonds on my fingers?" Heavenly asked.

Now I felt terrible. I mean, even if I wasn't sure I liked Heavenly, that didn't make me feel any better about hurting her feelings.

"It's not that," I said.

"Then what is it?" Heavenly asked.

Samara, Robby and I shared a guilty look. None of us knew what to say.

"Oh, all right, go ahead," Heavenly said. "I'd really hate to embarrass you."

Chapter

10

You might think that at some point during that day in school I would wonder a bit more about Heavenly Litebody and how she'd wound up in our kitchen that morning. But I didn't. From the moment I got to school, the only thing I thought about was eighth period, the last period of the day. I had American history eighth period and today was the day Mr. Hopewell, our history teacher, was going to assign us partners in our history project.

I wanted Roy Chandler to be my history partner. He, Jessica Huffington, and I were the only ones in the class who'd chosen to do our projects on the Great Depression of the 1930s.

The truth was, I'd had a crush on Roy Chandler for years. I secretly believed he was a good choice for a girl like me. He wasn't the sort of boy you would instantly pick out of a crowd. He was slightly built and average height, which meant he was a few inches shorter than me, with light-brown hair and lively eyes. And while I knew he was a good soccer and lacrosse player, he definitely wasn't one of the star athletes.

But once you got to know Roy, you realized that he was very smart and very funny. He was the kind of boy you could really have fun sitting next to on a field trip. But he wasn't the kind of boy you'd have to worry about some other girl stealing.

At least, not until Jessica Huffington came along.

"So today's the big day, huh?" said my friend Darcy Shultz at lunch. She was one of my closest friends. She had long black hair that she parted in the middle, a cute upturned nose, and a major set of braces. Her father was a history professor at a college and her mom was the president of the Soundview Manor Historical Society. In other words, the Schultzes were heavyweights in the brain department. And Darcy was no exception.

"Who do you think's going to win?" she asked. "You, or 'Have It All' Huffington?"

That was the nickname we'd given to Jessica, who was sitting at the "snob" table two rows away. We called her that because her family was very rich and she always got everything she wanted. As I said before, we lived in a pretty nice town and almost everybody got to go away on a vacation at least once a year. But only Jessica went away *every* vacation. She and her parents had literally been all around the world. And, she had to remind you, they always traveled first class.

Not only that, but Jessica had her own charge cards and cell phone with unlimited calling time. She was the only girl I knew who had already decided what kind of car her parents were going to give her when she got her driver's license.

"I just hope Mr. Hopewell picks me," I told Darcy. "I mean, can you believe Jessica's nerve? She never even knew Roy *existed* until she found out I wanted to be his partner on the project. And now she has to have him all to herself."

"It's not fair," Darcy agreed.

"And you can bet that as soon as the project is over she'll drop him like a stone," I added.

"Uh-oh," Darcy said, looking past me.

I turned in my seat. Jessica had gotten up from the "snob" table and had gone over to the table where Roy was sitting with some of his friends. She was smiling and talking to him and he was smiling back. Meanwhile, all the girls at the "snob" table and all the boys at Roy's table

had stopped talking and were watching the two
of them. A streak of jealousy as broad and green
as a field of corn raced through me.

"I bet I know what *that's* all about," Darcy
said.

"I could kill her," I grumbled.

"Maybe you should get over there and join
them," Darcy suggested.

"Get real. That would be way too obvious."

"Then what are you going to do?" Darcy
asked.

"I don't know," I answered, turning back to
my lunch before Jessica noticed I was staring.
I'd brought the white bag lunch from home that
Heavenly made.

"I thought you always bought lunch at
school," Darcy said.

"Usually," I answered.

"You finally got tired of mystery meat?" she
guessed.

I shook my head. "Tyler's new nanny packed
this for me. I mean, she's not really Tyler's new
nanny. She just thinks she is."

Darcy gave me a funny look. "What are you
talking about?"

I told her the story of how the nanny had
quit the night before after Tyler put Puff in the
clothes dryer (luckily the heat was off). And
how we'd all woken up that morning and
found this person named Heavenly Litebody in

the kitchen. And how even though we had no idea how she got there, she insisted she was Tyler's nanny. And how she'd cooked breakfast and made us all bag lunches.

"Litebody?" Darcy said. "How do you spell it?"

"I don't know; why?"

Darcy twirled a long strand of black hair around her finger. "I could swear I've heard that name before. Not the Heavenly part, but the Litebody. I just can't remember where. So how's the sandwich?"

I'd just taken a bite. "Know what?" I said, a bit surprised at how tasty it was. "It's a lot better than mystery meat."

Chapter

11

Know what it's like when you wait all day for something and then it doesn't happen? I waited all day on pins and needles for eighth period only to find out that Mr. Hopewell was absent. The substitute didn't know anything about picking partners for the history project and said we'd have to wait until the next day when Mr. Hopewell came back.

Darcy was waiting for me in the hall after class.

"So what happened?" she asked eagerly.

"Nothing," I answered, and told her about Mr. Hopewell being absent.

"Maybe you were lucky," she said as we started down the hall. "Now you'll have a chance to convince Roy that he should be your partner and not Jessica's."

"How?" I asked.

"I don't know," Darcy said. "Think of a good excuse for calling him tonight."

I spent the rest of the school day trying to think of a reason to call Roy. When school ended, Samara and I walked over to the elementary school and waited for Robby to come out. Then the three of us walked home together. Chance always went to one of his friends' homes after school. He rarely came home before dinner.

"Think she'll still be there?" Robby asked as we walked along the tree-lined sidewalk toward our house.

"She better be," I said. "Otherwise, who's been watching Tyler all day?"

"I can't believe Mom and Dad would hire someone who looked like her," Samara said.

That's when I realized that Samara didn't know the story about Robby finding Heavenly at InstantNanny.com.

"Do you know what that means?" Samara gasped after I'd told her. "If Robby hired her, he can fire her!"

Robby quickly shook his head. "No way, I'm scared of her."

Samara turned to me. "Would you fire her, Kit?"

"Negative," I said. "She scares me, too."

"You're both such chickens," Samara said.

"Oh, yeah?" said Robby. "Then *you* fire her."

Samara was quiet for a moment. "I know! Why don't we all get together and fire her?"

"Who'll watch Tyler tomorrow?" I asked.

"You could, Kit," Samara said.

"Why me?" I asked.

"Because you're the oldest," Samara said.

"What about Chance?" I asked. "He's two years older than me."

"Chance doesn't count," Samara said. "He'd probably go off with his friends and forget about Tyler. Besides, you get good grades in all your classes, Kit. It wouldn't matter if you skipped a day."

It wouldn't matter, except that Mr. Hopewell was almost certain to be back in school tomorrow. And if I wasn't there, I had no doubt who Roy Chandler's partner for the history project would be.

"I can't stay home tomorrow," I said. "I really have to go to school."

"Then how about this? Mom and Dad are supposed to come home tonight," Samara said. "One of them will have to stay with Tyler."

I winced at the thought. The only time we ever saw our parents really fight was when a nanny suddenly quit and one of them had to stay home and take care of Tyler until a new nanny could be found. Both of our parents were so busy with their jobs that they always insisted they couldn't miss a single day of work.

"I don't know, Samara," I said a little nervously. "Firing Heavenly could be more trouble than it's worth."

When we got home, Fortuna, the cleaning lady, was coming down the front walk with tears in her eyes. Fortuna was a short woman with black hair. She came to clean our house every other day. She usually arrived around noon, but rarely left before dinnertime.

We stopped on the front walk. "Fortuna, what's wrong?" I asked.

"You hired a new cleaning lady?" she asked as she wiped the tears from her eyes.

"No," I said.

"Then who cleaned the house?" Fortuna asked with a sniff.

It took a moment for me to figure out. "We've got a new nanny."

"Temporarily," Samara added.

"She thinks she's a cleaning lady," Fortuna complained. "I got here and she'd already cleaned almost the whole house. There was nothing left for me to do except some laundry and ironing."

"She's new and she doesn't understand," I said. "We'll talk to her, okay?"

"Thank you," Fortuna said with a sniff. "Next time I come back I hope the house is a big mess like usual."

"I promise," I said.

Fortuna said good-bye and went down the front walk. Robby, Samara and I continued toward the house.

"We never had a nanny who cleaned before," Robby said.

"She's not supposed to," I said. "You know how Mom feels. Since she and Dad can't be around to raise Tyler, she wants the nanny to be with him full time."

"Then why do they let him watch TV all day?" Robby wondered.

"Oh, come on, Robby, that's how *most* parents raise kids these days," Samara said.

But when we let ourselves into the house, Tyler wasn't watching TV. He was laughing happily as Heavenly gave him a horsey ride around the living room.

"Horsey jump! Horsey jump!" he chirped and banged her on the head with his pudgy little fist.

"You better not hit me or I'll start to buck!" Heavenly laughingly warned him. I was pretty sure she hadn't heard us come in.

"Buck, buck!"

Heavenly started to buck. Tyler laughed and laughed. Finally she rolled over and gently spilled him onto the living room floor. They both lay there laughing until they suddenly noticed us standing by the front door.

Heavenly sprang to her feet. The smile was gone.

"All right, you three," she said. "Into the kitchen. Get to work."

"Work in the kitchen?" Robby said.

"You've got homework, don't you?"

"I do my homework in my room," Samara replied.

"Right. With the television and the radio on," Heavenly said with a snort. "From now on we'll do it at the kitchen table. Then maybe you'll learn something."

Samara crossed her arms stubbornly. "You can't make me. In fact, we're firing you."

"Fine, I'm fired," Heavenly said. "Now let's get to work."

"No." Samara defied her. "I mean it. You're fired. You can pack your bags and go."

"Horsey no go! Horsey no go!" Tyler wrapped his arms around Heavenly's leg and hugged it tightly.

"Looks like someone in this family doesn't want me to go," Heavenly said.

"Well, I do," Samara snapped. "And so do Robby and Kit."

Heavenly gave Robby and me curious looks. The next thing I knew, we were both backing away from Samara.

"I'm not really sure," I said.

"Neither am I," agreed Robby.

Samara put her hands on her hips and glared at us. "You two are such wimps!" Then she spun around and faced Heavenly again. "You're still fired. And when Chance comes home I'm going to help him throw you out. And until then I'll be in my room watching all the TV and listening to all the radio I want!"

Samara picked up her maroon backpack and marched toward the stairs. Out of the corner of my eye, I saw Heavenly reach toward her left ear. Samara got to the bottom of the stairs. Just as she lifted her foot onto the first step, the bottom seam of her backpack split open and all her books fell to the floor.

"What the . . . ? Oh, darn!" Samara pulled off the torn backpack and then bent down and started to pick up her books. She always had to have the heaviest backpack of all of us. It seemed as if she had to bring home every single textbook, ring binder and notebook every day.

We watched as she struggled to gather up all the books that had fallen to the floor. But no matter how hard she tried, she couldn't handle them all at once. After a few books, she'd always get to the point where they'd start slipping out of her grasp just as soon as she added the next one.

"Would someone please help me?" she asked in frustration.

Robby and I both looked at Heavenly.

"I'm sure someone would help you get all those books into the kitchen," she said. "And I'd be glad to stitch up that backpack for you."

Instead of answering, Samara gave Heavenly the evil eye and once again tried to pick up all her books. It was sort of funny to watch them fall out of her arms almost as fast as she could pick them up.

Gla-thump! Finally she gave up and let them all fall to the ground.

"Oh, all right!" she cried in frustration. "I'll do my stupid homework in the stupid kitchen."

Heavenly smiled and turned to Tyler. "Want to help carry your sister's books into the kitchen?"

"I carry book." Tyler waddled over to Samara and picked up a notebook.

Tyler carried the notebook like a lunch tray in front of him. I couldn't help noticing that Samara was able to carry all her other books on her own into the kitchen.

Chapter

12

Doing homework in the kitchen wasn't so bad. We had a long wooden kitchen table that could easily fit a dozen people so there was plenty of room to spread out books and papers. And Heavenly gave us all milk and cookies for a snack.

While we did our homework, and Tyler played with his plastic toolbox, Heavenly got a needle and thread and began to sew the bottom seam of Samara's backpack.

"What are you doing?" Samara asked.

"Fixing it," Heavenly replied.

"Don't bother," Samara said. "I'll just get a new one."

Heavenly frowned. "But there's nothing wrong with this one. Except for the split seam it's practically brand new."

"I'm tired of that color," Samara said. "I want a black one."

"How long have you had this one?" Heavenly asked.

"About a month," Samara answered.

"That's ridiculous," Heavenly said. "Your parents shouldn't have to get you a new one just because you don't like the color anymore."

"They don't care," Samara said.

Ding Ding Dong! The doorbell rang.

"Anyone know who that is?" Heavenly asked.

Robby looked at the date on his watch. "Wes."

"Who?" said Heavenly.

"Our piano teacher," Samara groaned.

"You're first," I said to her.

"Do I have to?" Samara whined. "I just sat down."

"He always wants to get you out of the way first." Robby grinned. "So he can save the best for last."

Samara wrinkled her nose at him and started to get up. "You're so full of yourself." She left the kitchen.

"What was that all about?" Heavenly asked after Samara left.

"Samara never practices," Robby was eager to explain. "So Wes tries to get her out of the way first."

"Who goes next?" Heavenly asked.

I raised my hand.

"And you go last?" Heavenly said to Robby.

"Yeah, because I practice the most," Robby said.

"And Chance?" Heavenly asked.

"Chance doesn't play," Robby said. "He quit a long time ago."

Heavenly nodded quietly. From the living room came the jarring sounds of someone playing a piano badly. Heavenly grimaced.

"We'll have to see if we can't get Samara to practice," she said.

Robby and I glanced at each other. I wondered if he was thinking what I was thinking: that no other nanny had ever cooked for us, or sewn things, or cared whether we practiced piano. Heavenly seemed to want to do everything. That reminded me of something.

"When we came home before, Fortuna was really upset," I said. "She said you cleaned up the house."

"Tyler took a nap," Heavenly explained.

"But if you do Fortuna's job there'll be nothing for her to do," I said.

Heavenly gave me a blank look for a moment. Then she nodded. "That wouldn't be fair."

The kitchen door swung open and Wes came in. As I said, Wes was our piano teacher. His full name was Wesley Percifal Shackelford III, but he hated that. At one time the Shackelfords had owned almost all of Soundview Manor. Over the years they'd sold off a lot of it, but they were still one of the richest and best-known families around.

Wes was tall and had blond hair. The best way I can describe him is "almost handsome." If his nose had just been a shade smaller, and his eyes not quite so deep-set, and if his jaw only jutted out a little less, he would have been truly handsome. But he definitely was a nice-looking man and very sweet, too.

You could tell that Wes was the kind of person who'd been brought up with very good manners, so I was surprised when he just stood in the middle of the kitchen and stared at Heavenly.

"Wessy!" Tyler jumped up and waddled toward him. "Go for a ride, Wessy!"

Tyler sat down on Wes's foot (Wes had big feet) and wrapped his arms and legs around Wes's ankle. Usually when he did that, Wes would walk around. Tyler would cling to his foot and squeal happily. But today Wes didn't budge. He was still staring at Heavenly.

"Uh . . ." Wes opened his mouth to say something, but nothing came out. When Wes was nervous he tended to stammer and forget words. "You must be new."

"That's right." Heavenly looked down and continued sewing Samara's knapsack.

"Ride, Wessy! Ride, Wessy!" Tyler rocked back and forth on Wes's foot. Wes glanced at Robby and me.

"Oh, uh, Heavenly Litebody, meet Wes Shackelford," I said.

Heavenly's head suddenly popped up. She blinked. *"The* Shackelfords?"

"Well, I . . . guess." Wes nodded sheepishly.

"Oh." Just as quickly as her head had popped up, Heavenly ducked back down and concentrated on her sewing.

"Ride, Wessy!" Tyler called insistently.

"Okay, Tyler." Wes started around the kitchen table, swinging his leg while Tyler clung to his foot.

"Weeeeeeee!" Tyler screeched with joy. Meanwhile, Wes kept his eyes on Heavenly.

"Heavenly Litebody?" he said. "That's a very, um . . ."

"Interesting?" I guessed for him.

"Right," Wes said. "Interesting name."

Heavenly nodded without looking up.

"Where are you from?" Wes asked as he swung Tyler along.

"Nowhere important," Heavenly answered.

Wes glanced again at Robby and me.

"She won't tell us," I said.

"We don't even know how she got here,"

Robby added. "We just woke up this morning and here she was."

"What happened to, uh . . . ?" Wes asked. We knew he meant our last nanny.

"She quit last night," I said.

"Tyler put Puff in the dryer," Robby said. "I bet you didn't know cats can throw up twice their own body weight when they get dizzy."

"No, I can't say I did," Wes replied. "But I'm glad she's gone. I didn't like *her* at all." He stooped and looked down at Tyler. "This ride's over, bud."

"No! More! More!" Tyler insisted.

"That's all for now," Wes said firmly. Without another word, Tyler climbed off his foot and went back to playing with the plastic toolbox.

Wes went over to the sink and started to refill his water bottle from the tap. Wes always came to our house with a water bottle and took sips from it while he taught. As he filled the bottle, he kept sneaking glances at Heavenly from over his shoulder.

He finished filling the bottle and snapped the cap back on. He started to leave the kitchen, but stopped by the door.

"Well, Miss Litebody," he said, "it was very, er . . ."

"Nice to meet you?" I guessed for him.

"You too," Heavenly replied curtly. She

bobbed her head but didn't look up from her sewing.

Wes scowled for a moment, then went back into the living room to continue the lesson with Samara.

"You weren't very friendly," I whispered to Heavenly as soon as the kitchen door swung shut.

Heavenly raised her head and looked surprised. "I wasn't?"

"Wes was trying to be nice and you practically ignored him."

"I didn't mean to," she said.

"Then how come you didn't act friendlier?" I asked.

Heavenly shook her head as if she didn't have an answer. "Is he really a Shackelford?"

"As far as we know," I said. "Why?"

"Why does he teach music?" Heavenly asked.

"We don't know," Robby said. "We think he just likes to."

"Strange," Heavenly muttered, more to herself than to us. "Very strange."

It wasn't long before Samara came back into the kitchen. "Your turn," she said to me.

I went into the living room. Wes was sitting in a chair next to the piano bench.

"Did you practice this week, Kit?" he asked

59

as I sat down. Out here in the living room he seemed much less nervous.

"A little," I said.

"Hmmm." Wes rubbed his big chin in a slightly disapproving way. "Let's see how you do."

I played the piece I'd been working on.

"Well, all right," Wes said. "That shows some improvement."

We worked together for another twenty minutes and then Wes said, "Good, now how about promising me you'll practice twenty minutes a night?"

"I promise," I said, even though I knew I wouldn't. I started to get up. "I'll go get Robby."

"Wait a minute," Wes said in a low voice. "Tell me about er . . ."

"Heavenly?" I guessed.

"Right."

"What about her?"

"You really don't know where she came from?"

I shook my head. "Not a clue. She just appeared this morning. I still can't figure out how she got past the alarm system."

"Do you like her?" he asked.

"I don't know. I *sort of* like her, but she's really strict. I don't think Samara or Chance like her much."

"Hmmmm." Wes rubbed his chin again.

"Why do you want to know?" I asked.

"Just, er . . ."

"Curious?" I guessed.

"Right," Wes said. "How about Tyler; does he like her?"

"Yes, he likes her the best. A lot more than any of the other nannies we've had."

"Good." Wes smiled. "I'm glad to hear that."

"Why?" I asked.

"Oh, no reason. I just think she's . . . er . . . nice, that's all."

Suddenly I understood. "You *like* her!"

"No!" Wes sort of yelped. "And keep your . . . er . . ."

"Voice?"

"Right. Keep your voice down or she'll hear us."

"You do like her!" I whispered. "That's why you want to know if *we* like her. You're trying to figure out if she's going to stay."

Wes pursed his lips and gave me a serious look. "Promise me you won't . . ."

"Say anything?" I nodded eagerly.

"And the truth is . . . I don't know if I like her or not," he said. "All I know is, there's a . . . er . . ."

"Possibility?"

"Right." Wes nodded.

I couldn't help smiling.

"Stop . . . er . . . doing that!" Wes stammered. "And go get your brother."

Chapter

13

After Robby's lesson, Wes stopped in the kitchen to say good-bye. Once again, Heavenly hardly said a word to him.

At five o'clock Heavenly told us to take a break for an hour before dinner. It felt sort of strange to be put on a schedule. No one had ever done that before. But I can't say I really minded.

Chance came home just as we were sitting down for dinner. One of his eyes was purple and blue and swollen. There were flecks of dried red blood around his nose. His hands were scraped and dirty and the left knee of his pants was ripped.

It wasn't the first time he'd come home in that condition. Heavenly looked up from the kitchen counter where she was whipping a big bowl of mashed potatoes.

"You win?" she asked.

"Darn right," Chance answered.

Heavenly let out a big sigh and shook her head disapprovingly. "Go clean yourself up."

Chance headed upstairs. Almost immediately, the phone started to ring. No one moved to answer it.

"Isn't someone going to answer it?" Heavenly asked.

"It's for Chance," I said.

"How do you know?" Heavenly asked.

"Because they always start calling around now," I explained. "They" were girls and it was like they had radar or something. They always seemed to know just when Chance got home.

"You just let it ring?" Heavenly asked with a frown.

"You can take a message," I said, "but Chance'll never return the call."

"Why not?" Heavenly asked.

"I don't know," I said. "You'll have to ask him."

A little while later Chance came downstairs. He'd taken a shower and changed into clean clothes. His wet hair was plastered down on his head. Heavenly gave him a piece of paper with the names of three girls who'd called.

"What's for dinner?" Chance asked, crumpling the paper up and shooting it into the garbage can. "Nothing like a good fight to bring out an appetite."

"First we'll all sit," Heavenly announced, joining us at the dinner table.

"What for?" Chance asked.

"To give thanks."

"For what?" Robby asked.

"For living in a big warm house," Heavenly replied. "For having money for food and clothes and satellite television. For the good schools you go to. For having two parents who work hard to give you everything they can."

The rest of us stared at each other in wonder. No one had ever said anything like that to us before.

After a few moments, Heavenly got up and began to serve dinner. She had each of us bring our plate to the counter where she heaped it with meatloaf, mashed potatoes and peas. When she'd finished serving, she gave us each a glass of milk. Then she fixed a plate for Tyler and herself and sat down at the dinner table.

"I hate peas," Robby complained.

"Anyone who eats everything on their plate and practices piano for twenty minutes gets ice cream," Heavenly announced.

"What? Plain vanilla?" Samara turned up her nose. She'd been in a really bad mood ever since Heavenly had finished sewing her back-pack.

"Chunky Chocolate Cookie Dough Supreme," Heavenly replied.

Robby glumly lifted a forkful of peas. "Oh, well, here goes nothing."

Dinner actually went pretty well. Everyone was on their best behavior and even tried to use good table manners. Everyone except Samara ate everything on their plates.

"You know, I hate to be the one to say this," Samara said, "but nannies never eat dinner with us."

A silence settled over the dinner table. I waited for Heavenly to get mad, and I was surprised when she smiled. "It's my understanding that nannies never cooked dinner for you either. If I'm going to cook your dinner, the least I can do is eat it too."

"Well, you don't have to sit with us," Samara said.

"Shut up," Chance snapped.

Samara glared at him. "You're on her side too?"

"I don't know whose side I'm on," answered Chance. "But it's definitely not yours."

"I can't believe any of you," Samara muttered. "This total stranger appears in our house and you just let her take over."

The rest of us shared uncomfortable looks.

"Oh, I don't know," Robby finally said. "She doesn't seem much different from any of the *other* total strangers who've moved in and taken over before."

"And no offense or anything," I added, "but the only reason you're mad is because she fixed your backpack and now you don't have an excuse for getting a new one."

"Not to mention no Chunky Chocolate Cookie Dough Supreme because you didn't finish your dinner and probably won't practice piano," Chance said with a wry smile.

"It's just as well," said Samara. "I'm not the one who's going to get fat."

After dinner Heavenly made it clear that once again we were expected to help clean up. We listened to a lot of grumbling from Samara, but in the end she agreed to wipe down the table. Chance swept the floor. Robby scraped the dishes and I loaded them into the dishwasher. The funny thing was, when we all pitched in, it hardly took any time at all.

Heavenly said that after dinner there'd be more homework or "constructive time." That meant reading or drawing or playing games or an instrument or any computer game that didn't involve shooting or racing. This time both Robby and Samara argued that they'd miss their favorite TV shows. But Heavenly wouldn't budge. After a while Robby went into the living room to practice piano and Samara went up to her room (but only after Heavenly made her promise that she wouldn't watch TV).

I thought that Chance would also argue about having to do his homework at the kitchen table, but he seemed more amused than anything else. He'd actually brought a book home. Heavenly left us alone in the kitchen while she took Tyler upstairs to give him a bath and put him to bed.

After a few moments I looked up from my books and found Chance staring at me. Instantly I felt goose bumps racing down my sides.

"What?" I asked.

"Did anyone ever tell you that you're starting to get pretty?" he asked.

"No. But if it's true, then what was I before?"

Chance shrugged. "I don't know. Too young to count, I guess."

"Gee, thanks." I pretended to pout.

"Seriously," he said. "Maybe you're starting to lose some of your baby fat or something."

"Now, that's a compliment." I rolled my eyes toward the ceiling.

"Why can't you be serious?" he asked.

I could feel my jaw drop. "Look who's talking! You're never serious about *anything!*"

Chance frowned. "Sometimes I am."

He looked back down at his book. The conversation seemed to be ending. But I didn't want it to. Chance had never talked to me like this before. Like I was a real girl, and not just some annoying younger stepsister.

"So what happened to your eye?" I asked.

"Banged it on a door."

"Right." I couldn't help smiling. "That must have been some door. It gave you a bloody nose and tore a hole in your pants, too."

"Did you get the history project partner of your dreams?" Chance asked.

"Don't try to change the subject," I said.

"You're the one who's trying to change the subject," Chance shot back with a grin.

"For your information, Mr. Hopewell was absent and we didn't get assigned partners."

"Guess there's always tomorrow."

Tomorrow . . . That's when I remembered what had happened that day at lunch. Jessica "Have It All" Huffington was going to wreck my hopes and dreams if I didn't do something.

"Uh-oh, something's wrong." Chance must have read the expression on my face. Maybe it was for the best. I needed his advice.

"Listen, can you be serious for a second?" I asked.

"Doubtful."

"Please?"

"Oh, okay."

I told him what had happened that day and how I was worried that Jessica now had the advantage in the race for Roy. What I wanted to know from Chance was whether or not it would seem too obvious if I called Roy at home.

"Hmmmm, tough one." Chance leaned back and ran his fingers through his hair. Just then, Heavenly returned to the kitchen.

"Why don't we ask Heavenly what she thinks?" Chance suggested.

"No!" I didn't want the whole world to know. But it was too late. Before I could stop him, Chance told Heavenly the whole story.

"I see the problem," Heavenly said when he'd finished. "Let me think about it for a moment."

Chance turned back to me. "While she's thinking, you wouldn't know anyone who understands probability theory, would you?"

"If I remember correctly, it's the theory of estimating the probability of uncertain events," Heavenly said, touching her left hand to her left ear.

Chance turned back to her with a wide-eyed look. "You understand how it works?"

Heavenly smiled. "Got a deck of cards?"

"Uh, sure." Chance got up and went upstairs. Now that it was only Heavenly and me in the kitchen, I prayed that she'd remember to give me some advice about Roy. But before I could say anything, the phone rang.

Heavenly answered it. "Rand residence? Yes, who may I say is calling?" Heavenly put her hand over the receiver and held it out for me.

"Guess what?" she said in a whisper. "It's Roy Chandler."

Chapter

I took the phone but assumed she was kidding, of course. "Hello?"

"Kit? Hi, it's Roy."

For a moment I was so surprised I didn't know what to say. Heavenly motioned for me to take the phone into another room, so I told Roy to hold on.

It turned out that Roy wasn't sure what the science homework was that night. I told him, and then asked him what he thought about the history project.

"I've been reading about the Depression," he said. "I think Mr. Hopewell's right. It's too big for one person to cover alone."

"What part were you thinking of doing?" I asked.

"I like the part about the programs the government created to help people," Roy said. "Like the New Deal, and the WPA."

"That's funny," I said. "I want to write about how the Depression affected people. Like the dust bowl and the shantytowns. If we worked together it would fit really well."

"Sounds good," Roy said.

When we hung up I was so happy I practically skipped back into the kitchen. Inside, Heavenly was teaching Chance all about probability theory *by playing poker with him!*

"So you understand now that the chances of getting a pair in any five randomly picked cards is one in two?" Heavenly asked.

"Right," said Chance. "While the chances of getting three of a kind in the same situation is one in forty-seven. Wow, I can't believe I finally understand this stuff! And from playing poker!"

"Guess what?" I announced.

They both looked up from their cards.

"It's going to work!" I said. "I'm almost sure Roy and I are going to be partners!"

Just then Robby appeared in the doorway. "I ate dinner and practiced piano. Can I have my ice cream now?"

"All right," Heavenly said.

"Yahoo!" Robby cheered and headed for the refrigerator.

A few moments later, we were all eating bowls of Chunky Chocolate Cookie Dough Supreme.

"I hate to say this," I said, "but I feel bad about Samara."

Chance gave me an amazed look. "You *are* in a good mood!"

"Yeah," Robby agreed. "How could you feel bad about her?"

"Because we all got ice cream and she didn't," I said.

"She didn't finish her dinner or practice piano," Robby pointed out.

"But she never finishes dinner," I said. "And no offense or anything, Chance, but you didn't practice piano and you got ice cream."

"That's true," Chance admitted.

"You're right." Heavenly got up and went over to the intercom on the wall. She pushed the talk button and said "Samara?"

A moment later, Samara answered, "What?"

"You can come down and have some ice cream if you want," Heavenly said.

"Thanks, but I don't want to get fat," Samara answered curtly.

Heavenly came back to the table. "Well, I tried."

Robby put his empty bowl in the sink and then turned to us with one of his mopey faces.

"It's only eight o'clock and I'm bored. I did my homework and practiced piano. Why can't I watch TV?"

"Because most of what's on TV is mindless, senseless drivel," answered Heavenly.

"So what do *you* do when you're bored?" Chance challenged her.

"What do I do?" Heavenly got up and went into the living room. Dad recently had a huge entertainment center installed. It had a TV with a screen so big I could have stepped through it, and all sorts of video and DVD players. And coolest of all, it had surround sound that came out of speakers in the walls all around the room.

Heavenly pointed at the remotes lying on the living room table. "Can anyone figure out how to get MTV on this?"

"I thought you said TV is mostly mindless, senseless drivel," I reminded her.

"Absolutely," Heavenly replied, "but everyone needs a little mindless senseless drivel now and then."

Chance picked up one of the remotes and tried to make the TV go on. The entertainment center was new to all of us. When Chance got to MTV the picture came on before the sound. On the screen a group of heavily tattooed guys wearing black leather thrashed at their instruments and staggered around on the stage.

"Aw, it's just some dumb heavy metal show." Chance sounded disappointed.

"Great!" Heavenly cried. "Turn up the sound."

With a look of surprise Chance turned up the volume. The surround-sound speakers began to thump and throb loudly and I could actually feel the living room floor start to vibrate.

To our amazement, Heavenly began to dance and writhe wildly.

"Louder!" she cried.

Chance grinned and cranked up the volume—to the point where it almost hurt my ears. Then he tossed the remote on the living room table and turned to me. I watched his mouth move and knew he was asking if I wanted to dance, but the truth was the music was so loud that I never actually heard the words.

The next thing I knew, Chance, Heavenly and I were dancing around in front of the TV. The living room table was in the way so we moved it. Robby hopped up on the couch and pretended to be one of the musicians, jumping up and down, playing air guitar and swinging his head wildly.

I don't think more than a minute passed before Samara appeared at the bottom of the steps and stared at us as if we'd all gone mental.

Then Tyler came down the stairs in his pajamas. He was crying because we'd woken him. As soon as I saw him, I tapped Heavenly on the shoulder. She in turn tried to get Chance's attention. She wanted him to turn down the volume. But Chance was dancing by himself with his back to her.

And that's when the front door opened.

Chapter

15

Wearing their traveling coats and carrying their overnight bags, our parents stood in the doorway with shocked expressions on their faces. The music was still thundering. Tyler was still crying. Robby was still bouncing up and down on the couch and playing air guitar. Chance was still dancing with his back to us.

Heavenly quickly grabbed the remote and started pushing buttons. The TV changed to the Weather Channel. Robby stopped bouncing and Chance spun around. When he saw Mom and Dad he took the remote from Heavenly and turned everything off.

The music had been so loud that I could still hear it ringing in my head. Mom dropped her bags and scooped sobbing Tyler into her arms. Samara crossed her arms with a satisfied smile as if she hoped we'd all get into a ton of trouble. For a moment no one said a word. Mom and Dad surveyed the room, but their eyes kept coming back to Heavenly.

Finally Dad spoke. "Who are you?"

"Heavenly Litebody," she said.

"What are you doing here?" Dad asked.

"I am the nanny," Heavenly answered.

Dad and Mom shared a surprised look, then turned to the rest of us.

"Where is Emily?" Mom asked (Emily was our last nanny).

"She quit last night," Robby answered.

"Why?" Mom asked.

"Do you have to ask?" I answered. "Why do they all quit?"

Mom sighed and nodded, then turned to Heavenly again. "I'm sorry, but where did you say you came from?"

"She came from the Internet," Robby answered.

Mom and Dad both looked a little dumbfounded.

Robby told them the story about Instant-Nanny.com and how he'd left the emergency message, and how we'd found Heavenly in the kitchen that morning.

"Do you have any experience?" Mom asked Heavenly.

"Do you have any references?" asked Dad.

"Do you always dress like that?" asked Mom.

"Why were you playing the music so loud?" asked Dad.

"What is Tyler doing up at this hour and why was he crying?" asked Mom.

All those questions would have flustered me, but Heavenly just stood there with her hands in her back pockets. When the questions ended she simply said, "I believe I'm the right person for the job."

I don't think that was the answer my parents were expecting.

"Would you excuse us for a moment?" Dad asked. With Mom still cradling Tyler in her arms, they went into the kitchen to speak privately. Samara followed, no doubt eager to add her opinion.

Meanwhile, out in the living room, we started to straighten the furniture.

"What do you think is going to happen?" Robby asked in a low voice.

"Hard to say," answered Chance.

"With Samara in there you can bet Mom and Dad will get an earful," I said.

"Maybe we ought to go in there and say something too," Robby suggested.

But neither Chance nor I moved. I guess we still weren't sure how we felt about Heavenly. I definitely liked the meals she cooked, but I can't say I was thrilled about all the chores she made us do. And I knew Samara and the boys were upset that she wouldn't let them watch more TV.

After a while, Mom and Dad came back out of the kitchen. Tyler was still in Mom's arms, rubbing his sleepy eyes. Samara followed them. From the smug look on her face, I had a feeling I knew what Mom and Dad were going to say.

It was Dad who did the talking. "I'm sorry, Ms. Litebody, but we have no idea who you are or where you've come from. You may indeed be a very good nanny, but we have no way of knowing and under these circumstances we do not feel confident entrusting our children to you. So we would like you to leave."

A heavy silence fell over the living room. I wondered if Heavenly would try to argue or explain. The last thing in the world I expected was what she said next.

"You're making a mistake," she said.

Both Mom and Dad looked totally surprised. As I said, they were both important business people. They were used to telling people what to do. They definitely were *not* used to people telling them they'd made a mistake.

"Well, you may be right, Miss Litebody," Dad finally said. "But that is our decision."

"Then I'll go," said Heavenly. "But once I've gone I'll never come back."

Dad blinked in astonishment. Even Samara looked surprised. No one knew what to say.

Finally Heavenly nodded as if our silence had spoken loudly enough. "All right. If that's the way you want it. I'll go upstairs and get my bag."

Heavenly went upstairs, leaving the rest of us in the living room.

Samara was the first one to speak. She crossed her arms and nodded triumphantly. "Good—I'm glad we're getting rid of her."

Hearing her say that made me immediately jump to Heavenly's defense. "You know, she really wasn't that bad."

"She taught me how to play poker," Chance said.

"And she thinks we should get rid of the alarm system and get a big dog instead," added Robby.

"That's right," said Samara. "And you know what else she said? That people should sniff each other the way dogs do. Not only that, but she made us walk to school in the rain!"

From the looks on Mom and Dad's faces, I had a feeling we hadn't done a very good job of changing their minds.

A few moments later Heavenly came back down the stairs wearing her big bulky sweater and carrying a green canvas backpack. Without a word she crossed the front hall and stopped by the front door to punch the code in the keypad that deactivated the alarm.

Dad turned to us. "You told her our secret code?"

All four of us shook our heads. Meanwhile, Heavenly pulled the front door open and then looked back at us one last time.

"Horsey!" As if he suddenly understood what was happening, Tyler began to squirm out of Mom's arms. "Horsey! Horsey don't go!"

Tyler fought so hard that Mom couldn't hold him. She let him down. Tyler quickly waddled across the front hall and grabbed Heavenly's leg. "Horsey don't go! Horsey don't go!"

"Now, now, it's all right." Heavenly bent down and gently tried to pry his chubby arms from around her leg. "Mom and Dad will find another horsey to play with Tyler."

"*Nooooooooooooo!*" Tyler wailed and held on even tighter. "Horsey stay! Horsey don't go!"

It appeared that we'd reached a stalemate. Tyler clung to Heavenly's leg and refused to let go.

Mom and Dad shared a long, silent look.

"I think we need to discuss this some more," Dad said. Once again he and Mom went into the kitchen.

Samara's eyes went wide as she realized what was happening. She started to follow them.

"Hey!" Chance said sharply. "Leave them alone. They can think for themselves without you."

"Horsey don't go! Horsey don't go!" Tyler stayed stuck to Heavenly's leg like glue.

Once again we waited while Mom and Dad talked quietly in the kitchen. I noticed that the bright red ladybug was now crawling across the ceiling. Finally our parents came out.

"Due to the fact that Tyler seems to be rather . . . er . . . *attached* to you," Dad said to Heavenly, "we've decided to let you stay. But only until we can find a suitable replacement."

Mom kneeled down and held out her arms to Tyler. "It's okay, Tyler, honey. Miss Litebody can stay for a little while. Now come let Mommy put you to bed."

Still clinging to Heavenly, Tyler shook his head. "Horsey tuck me in."

Mom's face fell. "Oh, come on, hon, Mommy hasn't seen you for almost a whole week."

Tyler shook his head and squeezed Heavenly's leg tightly. I could see Mom's eyes start to grow watery.

Heavenly kneeled down until she was eye to eye with Tyler. "Listen, Mr. Wiggler, who's your mommy?"

Tyler pointed at Mom.

"Who loves you more than anyone in the world?" Heavenly asked.

Tyler hesitated for a moment, then pointed at Mom again.

"Who hasn't seen you in a long time and

misses you so much it hurts inside?" Heavenly asked.

Tyler looked at Mom, then aimed his pudgy little finger at her.

"Who really, really, *really* wants to give you a hug and a kiss and tuck you in tonight?"

"Mommy!" Tyler let go of Heavenly and waddled across the hall to Mom, who instantly scooped him up in her arms and carried him up the stairs.

Dad let out a long, deep breath and turned to Heavenly. "Thank you," he said. "We've got to unpack and settle in. We'll see you in the morning."

He went upstairs.

Chapter

16

It was late now, and the rest of us went to bed. Heavenly went up to the third floor, where the nanny's room was.

In my room, I changed into my pajamas and got into bed. I felt bad about Heavenly. She'd come out of nowhere and saved us in the middle of an emergency. She'd cooked and cleaned and worked really hard. Maybe we didn't like all her rules, but it seemed wrong to just send her away.

I got into bed, but couldn't sleep. That was pretty strange. Usually I can go right to sleep. But the more I thought about it, the more I felt we'd been unfair to Heavenly. Finally I knew there'd be only one way for me to get any sleep.

I slid out of bed and slipped on a sweatshirt. Because our house was big and old, it was hard to keep it heated, especially on the third floor at night. I quietly stepped out of my room and closed the door behind me.

Our house was shaped like an L. Robby, Samara, Chance and I had bedrooms on the second floor of the long wing. Our parent's bedroom and Tyler's nursery were in the second floor of the short wing.

The hall was dark. As I tiptoed toward the stairs at the center of the house, I could hear Dad and Mom snoring. They always came back from trips exhausted. Dad had a deep rough snore. Mom's was higher and more wheezy. It probably wasn't necessary to walk on tiptoes. It was doubtful I'd wake them up.

On the second floor landing where the two wings met was the door that led to the stairs to the third floor. I opened it slowly. The steps were dark. When I was younger I used to pretend that there were ghosts and giant spiders on the third floor. Even now I didn't like going up there in the dark. But I was afraid that if I turned on a light it might wake someone.

I started up the steps.

Then I looked up and almost had a heart attack!

There was someone at the top of the steps coming toward me!

"Chill out, it's just me," Chance whispered in the dark.

"You scared me." I put my hand over my

heart and felt it thumping in my chest. "What are you doing here?"

"What are *you* doing here?" Chance asked back.

"I felt bad and wanted to tell Heavenly I was sorry," I said.

"Yeah, me too."

"Did you?"

"She's not up here."

A thought struck me. "You don't think she's already left, do you?"

"No. I peeked in her room. Her backpack's still there."

"Then where do you think she is?"

"I don't know. Downstairs, maybe."

I turned around and started back down the steps. I could hear Chance's footsteps behind me. I took the stairs down to the first floor.

It was dark and cold on the first floor. At the bottom of the steps I stopped and looked around. It was hard to see.

"I don't think she's here," I whispered to Chance, who'd stopped beside me.

"Listen," he whispered back.

I held my breath. From the direction of the kitchen came the softest "clunk."

"Hear that?" Chance whispered.

I looked toward the kitchen door. There was no light seeping out from under it. "But it's dark," I whispered back.

"So?" Chance went past me and toward the kitchen. I have to admit I was glad he was there.

I followed as he slowly pushed open the door. Inside it was dark and quiet, but there was a certain scent in the air. It was that same sweet and sour, raspberry and lemon scent I'd smelled that morning.

"What's that?" Chance whispered.

"I don't know," I whispered back. "Herbal tea, maybe."

"Looking for someone?" Heavenly's voice caught us by surprise.

I jumped around and saw her silhouette. She was sitting in the dark at the end of the kitchen table.

"Why are you sitting in the dark?" I asked.

"Sometimes I like to," she answered.

"Think we could join you?" Chance asked.

"It's your house," Heavenly answered with a hint of sharpness in her voice.

Chance and I sat down with her in the dark. I don't know why we didn't turn on a light. I guess we figured she was there first and if she wanted the lights off, we should leave it that way.

For a few moments we sat without speaking. Heavenly picked up her mug and took a sip, then set it back down on the table with another little "clunk."

I finally began. "I just want to say I'm sorry."

"Why?" Heavenly asked.

"Because you came here to help us," I said. "And you *did* help us. And I don't think we've been very nice to you."

"That's the way I feel too," said Chance. "We should have stood up for you when Mom and Dad came home. Instead of just standing there like a couple of dolts."

"What's done is done." Heavenly's voice was flat.

"In a lot of ways you're the best nanny we've ever had," I said. "I mean, you're the only one who's ever acted like she cared. It seems like a shame that you have to go."

"You really want me to stay?" Heavenly asked.

"Yes, I think I do," I said.

In the dark, Heavenly shot a questioning look at Chance. "And you?"

Chance hesitated. "Why's it so important to you that we make our beds and do the dishes and stuff?"

"How old are you, Chance?" Heavenly asked.

"Sixteen."

"So in a few years you'll be finished with high school and going to college," Heavenly said.

"I don't know. Maybe."

"Even if you don't go to college, do you

intend to live here for the rest of your life?" Heavenly asked.

"No way!" Chance chuckled. "As soon as high school's over I'm out of here."

"Don't you think it would help if you knew how to take care of yourself?" Heavenly asked.

"I know how to take care of myself," Chance said.

Heavenly didn't reply. In the dark it was hard to read her face. It grew quiet again. I heard chair legs scrape as Chance stood up.

"I'm gonna get some sleep," he said. "I just wanted to say it was kind of cool having you around, Heavenly."

"Thanks, Chance," she said.

Chance turned to me in the dark. "You coming?"

"In a minute," I said.

Chance crossed the darkened kitchen and left. At the kitchen table Heavenly lifted her mug, took another sip and set it down.

"That smells really good," I said. I was sort of hoping she'd offer me some, but she didn't.

"I really am sorry," I said.

"Yes, I know," she said.

"I *mean* it," I said.

She didn't answer.

"Can I ask you a question?" I said.

"Go ahead."

"Where did you come from?"

"It doesn't matter," she answered.

"Maybe it does. If you told my parents—"

"No."

"Why not?"

"Because where I came from and how I got here isn't important," Heavenly said. "The only thing that matters is that I am the right nanny for this family. If your parents can't see that, it's their own fault."

"But they're gone most of the time," I said. "What about us kids? Don't we have the right to decide?"

"I thought you'd already decided," Heavenly said.

Just then the kitchen door creaked open. I assumed it was Chance coming back. A tiny beam from a little flashlight swept past the stove and stopped on the refrigerator. Heavenly and I watched silently as someone smaller than Chance crept toward the refrigerator and opened it. In the light from the refrigerator we watched Robby reach into the freezer compartment.

"Come to Poppa," he chortled to himself as he took out the container of Chunky Chocolate Cookie Dough Supreme ice cream.

"Ahem!" Heavenly cleared her throat loudly.

"Ahhhhh!" Robby yelped and dropped the ice cream on the floor. "Who's that?"

"Kit and Heavenly," I answered.

"You guys scared the snot out of me," Robby

blurted. He flicked on a light. Heavenly and I had to shield our eyes from the sudden brightness.

"Put the ice cream back," I said.

"Aw, come on, Kit," Robby whined.

"You don't need it, Mr. Chub."

"I *deserve* it after you guys scared me like that," Robby countered.

"Want me to tell Mom and Dad?" I asked.

"How about just a little?"

"No."

"Thanks a lot," Robby grumbled and put the ice cream back into the freezer. "What are you guys doing down here anyway?"

"Guarding the refrigerator."

"Really?"

"No, silly. We're talking."

"What about?" Robby asked.

"I was telling Heavenly I didn't want her to leave," I said.

"But Mom and Dad decided," Robby said.

"I know. But I wanted to tell her just the same. Do *you* want her to leave?"

Robby came over to the table. "I don't know. I mean, you did get us ice cream, but I hate having to eat peas to get it."

"In life you learn to take the bad with the good," Heavenly said. She lifted her mug to her lips. I noticed she had a small, round bright red tattoo on the inside of her thumb.

"And I don't think it's fair that we only get to watch an hour of TV a night," Robby complained. "I can't see all my favorite shows."

"Can I ask you a question, Robby?" Heavenly asked.

"Uh, sure."

"What were your favorite shows three years ago?"

"They were, uh, uhm, gimme a minute and I'll remember."

"They must have been really important," Heavenly said with a chuckle.

"They were," Robby insisted. "Just because I can't remember them doesn't mean anything."

"Maybe some ice cream would help your memory," Heavenly teased.

"Not funny," Robby muttered. "It probably wouldn't help me remember anyway. But remembering what my favorite shows were isn't the point. Watching TV relaxes me. It's hard being a kid. There's a lot of stress. Everyone needs some downtime."

Heavenly actually laughed. "Boy, you are a trip. I'll miss you, Robby."

"You will?" Robby replied, surprised.

"Oh, yes." Heavenly turned to me. "And I'll probably miss you, too, Kit."

Robby and I shared a look across the kitchen. It's funny how sometimes you know exactly what someone's thinking.

"Maybe you shouldn't go, Heavenly," I said.

Heavenly raised an eyebrow. "But I thought you didn't like my rules."

Robby and I shared another look.

"Maybe we could learn to like them," I said.

Just then the kitchen door swung open. Mom stepped in wearing a white robe and a puzzled, cross look on her face. "What in the world are you two doing up at this hour?" she asked Robby and me.

"Just talking," Robby answered.

"Talking? After midnight? You both have school tomorrow morning."

"So?" Robby asked.

"So?" Mom repeated, narrowing her eyebrows. "So you will go to bed right now, young man. And you, too, Kit."

She held the kitchen door open. As we passed her, I heard her say to Heavenly, "This may come as a surprise to you, Miss Litebody. But one of a nanny's most important jobs is to get children to bed at a reasonable hour, *not* to keep them up all night."

And then she closed the door.

Chapter

17

I went to bed that night certain that Heavenly would be leaving as soon as my parents found a replacement. But when I woke up I have to admit that my thoughts were more on Roy Chandler than who our next nanny would be. Once again, I worked extra hard on looking nice, picking out my second-best outfit (since I'd worn my best one the day before) and doing a little something extra with my hair and make-up.

Later, when I came out of my bedroom, I ran into Mom on the stairs. I assumed that Dad had already left for work. He always went in very early. But sometimes, when Mom had been away for a long time, she would stay home and have breakfast with us before going back to work.

"Tyler's not in the nursery," Mom said with a concerned look.

To me, that was good news. "I bet Heavenly took him down for breakfast."

As we went downstairs, the scent of breakfast was again in the air. Mom looked at me with a puzzled expression on her face.

"I told you," I said. "She cooks breakfast."

We went into the kitchen. Tyler was in his highchair. On a plate in front of him was some French toast cut into bite-size pieces. Robby was sitting at the kitchen table eating French toast. The kitchen table was set with plates, napkins and silverware. In the middle of the table were pitchers of orange juice and milk. Heavenly was over by the stove, making more French toast for the rest of us.

"Rench toast, Mommy!" Tyler held up a small square of French toast.

"I see," Mom said.

"What's with this orange juice?" Robby asked.

"Something wrong?" Heavenly asked from the stove.

"It tastes different," Robby said.

Heavenly held up an orange. "It's fresh squeezed. From real oranges."

"Well, it tastes good and everything," Robby said, "but what's all this stuff floating in it?"

"Pulp," Heavenly answered. "Some people

like it with their juice. If you don't, bring it over and I'll strain it out."

Robby brought his glass to the sink and watched while Heavenly strained out the pulp.

"This is quite a breakfast," Mom said.

"It's what children should have every day," Heavenly replied in a clipped tone.

The kitchen door swung open and Samara and Chance came in.

"Smells good," Chance said, picking up a plate and heading for the stove. Heavenly slid three pieces of French toast onto his plate. Samara took one piece.

"You're eating breakfast?" Mom asked in surprise as Samara carried her plate back to the kitchen table.

"Just a little," Samara answered sheepishly. "Heavenly says it's good for you."

"What about you, Kit?" Heavenly asked.

I picked up a plate and got my share of breakfast. Then I went over to the kitchen table and sat down with the others.

Meanwhile, Mom stood in the middle of the kitchen as if she wasn't certain what to do.

"Rench toast!" Tyler said, holding up a small square toward Mom. "You eat."

"Thank you, but I never have breakfast," Mom answered.

"Well, that explains that," Heavenly mumbled.

Mom frowned. "Sorry?"

"Nothing," Heavenly replied.

But Mom knew Heavenly had said something, and that whatever it was, it wasn't exactly nice.

"Since things seem to be under control," Mom said, "I guess I'll go."

She started out of the kitchen, then stopped. "I suppose I should explain the alarm system to you, Miss Litebody. In case you want to take Tyler out today."

"I'm familiar with the alarm system," Heavenly replied.

"But there's a code," Mom said.

"T, R, S, K, C," Heavenly recited.

With a surprised look on her face, Mom turned to us. "You weren't supposed to tell her."

"We didn't!"

"Then how could she possibly know?" Mom asked.

"We don't know," I said. "She just does."

Mom gave me a disbelieving look. "I'll see you all tonight," she said and left the kitchen.

As soon as she left, I asked Heavenly why she hadn't been friendlier to Mom.

"She wasn't very friendly to me last night," Heavenly answered.

"Yeah, but she's the mom," Robby said.

"What's that supposed to mean?" Heavenly asked.

"Well, uh, she's the boss."

"Oh, I see," said Heavenly. "Because she's the mom and I'm the nanny, that gives her the right to be mean to me?"

"She's not really mean," I said. "She's just really busy."

"So?"

"I think what Kit means is at work Mom's the boss," Chance tried to explain. "People do what she tells them to do. She's not real used to having an employee who doesn't do things her way or tells her what to do."

"Well, then I guess I won't be here for long," Heavenly said.

My eyes met Chance's. He glanced down at the table with a disappointed expression. It was strange. Considering how much he hated people telling him what to do, I would have thought he'd be glad to see Heavenly go. But like me, he wasn't.

After breakfast we cleaned up the kitchen. This time I scraped the dishes and Chance put them into the dishwasher. Samara and Robby finished sweeping the floor and clearing the table and went upstairs.

"Looking hot again, Kit," Chance said in a teasing voice after the others left.

"Stop it!" I whispered back.

"Hey, I mean it. I don't see how any guy could refuse you for a history partner."

"Thanks." I gave him a weak smile. I was keeping my fingers crossed.

A few minutes later Heavenly put Tyler into the stroller and buckled his little seat belt. The rest of us put on our jackets and coats and got our backpacks.

We gathered quietly in the hallway by the front door. No one said anything.

"Ready?" Heavenly asked.

We all nodded.

"Why's everyone so quiet?" she asked. "We're not going to a funeral."

"We might as well be," said Robby as he opened the front door and we filed out.

Outside it was a bright, sunny, but cold day. We started down the sidewalk toward school. Up ahead I saw a bunch of Chance's friends. Usually he'd run to catch up with them, but today he stayed and walked with us.

We passed the big houses of our neighborhood with their well-kept lawns and shiny cars parked in the cobblestone driveways.

"Still pretty quiet this morning," Heavenly observed.

Robby, Chance and I stole glances at each other. I had a feeling we were all thinking the same thing.

"Why can't you deal with Mom differently, Heavenly?" I asked.

"Why should I?"

"Because she's not used to being argued with," Robby said. "I mean, we can do it because we're her kids."

"But even then she doesn't like it," Chance added.

"But she really doesn't like it when someone else does it," I said.

"Why should I be nice to her if she can't be nice to me?" Heavenly asked.

"She'll change," I said.

"She just has to get used to you," said Robby.

"Used to me?" Heavenly repeated. "What does she have to get used to?"

Robby, Chance and I shared more glances. I knew what we were all thinking, but no one dared say it. No one, that is, except Samara.

"Well, she doesn't like the way you *look*, for one thing," Samara said.

"Doesn't like the way I look!" Heavenly repeated angrily. "What's wrong with the way I look?"

By now we were nearing the school again and all the fancy mothers and nannies were letting their children out of their fancy cars.

"Oh, yes, I forgot," Heavenly said as she looked at them. "Well, if you ask me, *they're* the ones who look strange. Like a bunch of malnourished life-size Barbie dolls."

Robby went into the elementary school. The next stop was the middle school. Samara saw a friend and ran off to talk to her. As Chance, Heavenly and I walked up the sidewalk, Mr. Hopewell hurried past, lugging his briefcase.

"Hello, Kit!" he waved.

"Hi, Mr. Hopewell." I waved back.

"Hopewell?" Chance said. "Isn't he your history teacher? The one who was absent yesterday?"

"Yes," I said.

"Then today's definitely your big day!" Chance said loudly. "The day of Roy!"

I winced. "Would you please keep your voice down? Everyone can hear."

"Hey, what's there to be embarrassed about?" Chance asked. "There's nothing wrong with young love."

"Chance!" I practically yelled. "Stop it!"

"Okay, see ya." Chance headed off toward the high school. I stuck my tongue out at him.

"Don't let him get to you," Heavenly advised.

"I just don't get what's with him," I muttered.

Heavenly smiled.

"What is it?" I asked.

"Well, this is just a guess," Heavenly cautioned. "But I think he's jealous."

"Jealous of what?" I asked.

"Roy Chandler."

"Why?" I asked.

"Because if Roy Chandler is lucky, he's going to get himself a very pretty history partner."

"No!" I cried. "That's the last thing I want. He can't get Jessica Huffington for a partner."

"Who's talking about Jessica Huffington?" Heavenly laughed.

"You."

"No, silly," Heavenly said. "I meant *you*."

Chapter

18

That afternoon after school, I went straight up to my room and locked the door. I turned the radio on low, then got into bed and pulled the blanket over my head. Maybe, if I was lucky, Heavenly would be so busy helping Robby and Samara with their homework that she wouldn't notice I was missing.

As far as I was concerned, I was going to stay in bed for the rest of my life.

For a while I thought I'd gotten away with it. Then I heard a knock on the door. "Kit?"

It was Heavenly.

"Go away," I said.

"What's wrong?"

"Nothing."

"Why aren't you downstairs doing your homework?"

I didn't feel like answering. Heavenly didn't answer all my questions. Why did I have to answer hers?

"Kit?"

"Go away," I said.

"Is something wrong?"

"No."

"Then why are you under that blanket?"

"It's none of your—"

Wait a minute! How did she know I was under my blanket? I pulled the blanket off my head.

Heavenly was standing by the door, inside my room!

"How did you get in?" I asked.

As usual, Heavenly ignored my question. "Do you want to tell me what's wrong?"

I shook my head. "No way! Forget it! This time I want to know how you did that. My door was locked!"

Heavenly came toward the bed. She had a soft, worried expression on her face. This was a side of her I hadn't seen before. "Tell me what happened."

"Not until *you* tell me how you got in," I insisted.

"I came through the doorway," she said.

"You couldn't have. The door is locked."

"No, it's not." Heavenly went back to the door and turned the knob. The door opened. "See?"

"That doesn't prove anything! It's supposed to open from the inside. It's only locked on the outside."

"Maybe you thought it was locked, but it wasn't," Heavenly said.

I let out a big sigh and pressed my lips together. I was positive I'd locked the door. But not so positive that I would have bet my life on it. Anyway, it didn't matter now.

Heavenly came back toward the bed. "So what's going on?"

I didn't want to tell her. I mean, she was still a stranger, and the way things looked, she wouldn't be staying with us much longer anyway. But that was another problem with having a mom who worked. It wasn't like I could call her at work and tell her how Jessica Huffington had snaked Roy from under my nose and gotten him for a history partner. I mean, I could try, and if Mom wasn't too busy she always tried to talk. But even when we started to talk, she would be interrupted by some urgent matter or phone call or meeting. Even when I could start a conversation with Mom at work, I could never finish it.

"Jessica Huffington got Roy for her history partner," I moped.

"How?"

Still sitting in bed, I drew my knees up under my chin and explained how Jessica somehow found out what part of the Great Depression I wanted to cover and then made sure she was covering the exact same thing!

"How do you know Roy didn't want her in the first place?" Heavenly asked.

"Because last night Roy and I talked about being partners," I said. "I thought we'd agreed. Then Jessica had to sneak behind my back. She's such a snake!"

A crooked smile crossed Heavenly's lips. "Now tell me the truth, Kit. Is it really that important to you?"

"You know what?" I answered. "It really is. I mean, it's not that I really, really have to have Roy for a partner. It's that Jessica took him away on purpose. She's so *competitive* and mean. It's like she does things not because she wants them, but just because she doesn't want you to have them. I just wish for once she didn't get her way."

Heavenly rested her chin on her fist. To tell you the truth, I was surprised. This was a completely different side of her. We'd never had a nanny for Tyler before who cared how the rest of us felt. It may sound strange, but just realizing that made me feel a little better.

"What do you think you can do about it?" she asked.

"I can't do anything about it," I pouted. "It's too late. Mr. Hopewell told them to work together on it. I'm just the old third wheel. The odd man out."

"Isn't there anyone else in the class you could be partners with?" Heavenly asked.

"Oh, Heavenly, of course there is," I said. "I mean, I'd have to change my project, but big deal. That's not the point. The point is that I've liked Roy for a really long time and this would have been the perfect thing for us. And the other point is that Jessica doesn't even care about him. She only did it to mess up my plans."

"Isn't there any other way you can get to spend time with Roy?" she asked.

I had to sigh. "Listen, Heavenly, do me a favor. Don't get all grown up and logical on me, okay? This is really simple. Girl likes boy. Girl was really looking forward to working with boy. Then girl gets tricked by Jessica 'Have It All' Huffington. Now girl is really, *really* disappointed, and wishes Jessica Huffington would choke on her cell phone. And that's the end of it."

Heavenly pursed her lips into a little smile. "Okay, that's the end of it. Now how about coming downstairs and doing your homework?"

I shook my head.

She got up. "What about dinner?"

"Doubtful."

"If that's what you want," Heavenly said. "I'll check in on you later."

She left the room. Suddenly I realized that she hadn't made me come downstairs to do my homework. Nor had she insisted I come for dinner. It was almost as if she really did understand how upset I was.

Chapter

19

I didn't come out of my room, except to go to the bathroom, for the rest of the night.

After dinner I heard a knock on my door.

"Go away," I said.

"Kit?" It was Chance.

"You heard me," I said. "Go away. What do you want anyway?"

"I want to talk," Chance said.

"No."

The doorknob clicked as Chance tried to turn it. But this time I'd made sure it was locked. "Come on, Kit, don't do this."

If it had been anyone else, I would have told them to get lost. But it was Chance. I was actually curious about what he wanted. So I went to the door and opened it a little.

Chance was standing in the hall with his

hands jammed in his pockets and a grim expression on his face.

"Guess you didn't get Roy for your history partner, huh?" he said.

"Guess not."

"Well, I just wanted to say I'm sorry about that," he said. "I mean, if there's anything I can do . . ."

"Like what?" I asked.

"I don't know," he said, but there was a glint in his eye. "Want me to get into a fight with someone? I'm pretty good at that."

I couldn't keep a smile off my face. "You want to fight Jessica Huffington?"

"Only if she's bigger and stronger than me," he said.

"Well, she's not. But thanks for offering."

"Anytime," Chance said.

"'Night, Chance."

"'Night, Kit."

I closed the door and pressed my back against it. Sometimes it was hard to know what to make of Chance. I mean, there was nothing he, or anyone else, could do about my problem. But just the same, I was touched by his offer.

Just before bedtime someone knocked again.

"That you again, Chance?" I asked.

"It's Heavenly."

"Come in," I said.

"I can't. The door's locked."

I got up and went to the door. "Funny, that didn't stop you before," I said as I let her in.

"Feel any better?" she asked, sitting down on the edge of my bed.

I shrugged. "A little, but not much. The worst part is thinking about school tomorrow. I just don't know how I'll even be able to look at Jessica without . . . I don't know . . . without either wanting to break down and cry or tear her eyeballs out."

"Maybe you'll be surprised."

"Right," I smirked. "And maybe you're the tooth fairy. Now get out of here."

"All right." She got up. "But just remember. Things have a way of changing."

"Anything you say," I answered as she crossed the room and started to open the door. But then I felt bad.

"Heavenly?" I said.

She stopped and looked at me. "Yes?"

"Thanks for stopping in."

She smiled. "Anytime."

The next day was Friday. Usually I was glad because it meant the weekend was coming. But that morning it didn't matter. All I knew was that I had to go to school and face Roy and Jessica. Somehow I managed to drag myself out of bed and get dressed. More than anything, I dreaded the superior look I knew I'd see on Jessica's face.

Robby and Chance were already eating breakfast. Heavenly had made pancakes. She was feeding Tyler. But everyone stopped eating when I got down to the kitchen.

"What?" I asked.

Without a word, Chance and Robby looked back down at their breakfasts. Heavenly gave me a questioning look. I gave her a shrug that said, "Hey, the show must go on."

I have to admit that the pancakes smelled really good. After skipping dinner the night before, I was awful hungry. In a way, I was a little disappointed in myself. In my head, I wanted to be so angry and upset that I still had no appetite. But my stomach disagreed strongly.

I gave in and went over to the counter and filled my plate with pancakes. That bright red ladybug was crawling across the counter.

This bug sure gets around, I thought as I carried my plate to the kitchen table and sat down with the boys.

"Feeling better?" Chance asked.

"No, just hungry," I answered and started to eat.

"Hey, Kit," Robby said, "did you hear about the kid who swallowed three quarters, four dimes and five pennies?"

"No."

"He got a really bad stomachache. So his parents took him to the doctor's office and waited while they X-rayed him. When the doctor finally came out of the office, the parents rushed over to him and said, 'Did you see any change in our son?'"

"So?" I grumbled.

"Change, Kit," Chance said. "Quarters, dimes, pennies . . . get it?"

"Ha ha," I muttered.

"Maybe we ought to leave her alone," Heavenly said.

Samara came down and had some breakfast. As usual she was too self-absorbed to notice anything unusual.

A little while later we all left for school. Outside, Chance and Samara ran off to catch up with their friends. Heavenly, with Tyler in the stroller, and I dropped Robby at the elementary school.

"You really don't have to walk me to the middle school," I told Heavenly. "To tell you the truth, I think I'd rather go the rest of the way alone."

"All right," Heavenly said. "Just try to be cheerful, okay?"

"What do I have to be cheerful about?"

Heavenly reached up to her left ear. "Strange things happen just when you least expect it."

"Oh, right." I pretended to slap my head. "How could I forget? You're the tooth fairy."

"You never know." Heavenly winked and turned the stroller back down the sidewalk.

Maybe Heavenly didn't know, but I did—that today was going to be one of the worst of my life. I walked into the middle school just as the bell rang, and went down the hall to my locker. Maybe, if I was lucky, Jessica would be out with the flu. Maybe, if I was *really* lucky, she and her family had moved overnight to Nome, Alaska.

No such luck. As I closed my locker, who should I see coming down the hall toward me? Roy and Jessica, of course.

I felt myself stiffen. The last thing I wanted was for them to see me. Not knowing what else to do, I quickly opened my locker again and kneeled down as if I was looking for something. Meanwhile, out of the corner of my eye, I could see Jessica and Roy coming closer. Finally the moment came when I had to turn away completely or they would have seen me watching them.

Now it would just be a matter of waiting for them to pass.

"Kit?" When Jessica said my name I felt my stomach twist into a knot. A hot flush spread over me like a fever. I looked up over my shoulder and pretended to be surprised.

"Oh, hi," I said, straightening up. What could

she possibly want? I wondered. And why was Roy standing there with a smile on his face?

"Roy and I were talking last night," Jessica said. "And we realized that there's an awful lot more to the Great Depression than we ever expected."

"It's not just about the people who lost their jobs and were poor," Roy added. "And it's not just about what the government did to fix it."

"There's also the whole part about how it started in the first place," said Jessica.

Why are you both telling me this? I wondered.

"Anyway, I think we both felt kind of bad that Mr. Hopewell paired us together and left you out," Roy went on. "So we just stopped by his classroom and asked if we could make it a three-way project and include you as the third partner."

"But only if you want to," Jessica added. "We don't want to force you or anything. We just thought it would be really neat if you would do the part about how the Depression affected the people of our country."

"But I thought that was the part you wanted to cover," I said.

"It was," Jessica admitted, "but Roy said you really wanted to do it. And I don't care that much. So if it's okay with you I'll do the part about what caused the Depression in the first place."

"And that way we'll really have the Great Depression covered," added Roy.

Can you blame me if I felt just a little bit shocked? It took me a moment, but I said yes.

"Great," Roy said. "Why don't we get together in the library at lunch and plan it out?"

I said I'd be there. Then the bell rang. It was time to go to class.

My next class was gym. I went into the girls' locker room and sat down on the bench in front of my locker. I started to do the combination on the lock, then stopped. A bright red ladybug was crawling across my locker.

"Hey, what's up?" It was Darcy. Her gym locker was a few down from mine.

"The weirdest thing just happened," I said, and then told her all about Jessica and Roy asking me to be their partner in the history project.

"That's great," Darcy said.

"Come on, Darcy," I said. "When did you ever know Jessica 'Have It All' to want to share anything?"

"Well . . ." Darcy hesitated. "Maybe she's changed."

Maybe she's changed, I thought. Maybe Darcy was right. But it was strange how many things had "changed" since Heavenly Litebody "magically" appeared in our kitchen. I began to think about the other strange things that had happened. Like the tabs on the soda cans that kept breaking off when Chance tried to disobey Heavenly. And how the doorknob had come off in his hand when he tried to sneak out. And how the seam on Samara's almost brand-new backpack had suddenly split when she tried to go upstairs against Heavenly's wishes. And these ladybugs.

And to top it all off, Heavenly *still* hadn't explained how she knew the secret code for the alarm!

A bell rang.

"Uh, Kit," Darcy said, "if you don't get into your gym clothes fast you're going to be late."

"Right." As I started to do the combination on my lock, I made a decision. I was going to watch Heavenly a whole lot closer from now on.

That night Heavenly made us dinner. She sat at the table and fed Tyler, but she didn't eat with us.

"Here's a riddle," Robby said. "What do you get when you cross a parrot and a centipede?"

"I don't know," I said.

"A walkie-talkie." Robby grinned.

"It would be really nice to eat dinner without listening to your stupid jokes," Samara complained.

"Get stuffed," Robby muttered.

"Here's another riddle," I said. "What does knowing our secret alarm code, tabs breaking off soda cans, doorknobs coming off doors, backpacks splitting open, and Kit being asked to work on a certain history project all have in common?"

At first everyone looked puzzled, but slowly, they figured out what I was getting at. It wasn't long before we were all looking at Heavenly.

"What are you looking at me for?" Heavenly asked. "I don't know."

"Somehow I think you're behind them all," I said.

"How could that be?" Heavenly asked.

"That's the part I haven't figured out yet."

Heavenly smiled. "Let me know when you do. In the meantime, make sure you clean up your dishes and straighten up the kitchen." She stood up and lifted Tyler out of his highchair. "I'm taking Tyler up for his bath."

"How come you didn't eat with us?" Robby asked.

"Because I've got better things to do," Heavenly answered and left.

"Better things?" Robby wondered out loud after she was gone.

"Probably some TV show she wants to see," Chance guessed.

"She doesn't watch TV," I reminded him.

"She's weird," Samara announced. "She acts weird, she thinks weird and she dresses weird."

"Look who's talking," I said. "The pillar of normalcy."

"What's a pillar?" Robby asked.

"Isn't it one of those tall things in the front of some houses?" Chance asked.

"You mean a column," said Samara.

"What's that got to do with Samara?" Robby asked.

"Forget it," I said.

We finished dinner and cleaned up the kitchen. By now, everyone knew their jobs and did them without complaining or arguing. But this was the first time we'd ever done it without Heavenly standing over us.

Since it was Friday night, everyone except Chance sat down in the living room to watch TV. Chance went upstairs to go online and talk to his friends on his computer.

A little while later Heavenly came downstairs wearing her baggy sweater and a brown over-the-shoulder bag. She left the bag by the front door and sat down with us on the couch to watch TV. I noticed that she'd put on make-up and fixed her hair. And instead of wearing pants, she was wearing leggings and a short skirt.

"You look nice," I said.

"Thanks."

"Are you going out?" I asked.

"You don't think I dressed up just for you?" Heavenly asked with a smile.

"Do you have a boyfriend?" asked Robby.

"Maybe," answered Heavenly before I could tell him that it was none of our business.

"I bet Wes would like to be your boyfriend," said Samara.

"Who?" Heavenly asked.

"You know, our piano teacher," Samara said.

"Oh, him." Heavenly rolled her eyes. "What makes you think he wants to be my boyfriend?"

"Just the way he looks at you," Samara said. "He forgets to teach piano and just stares at you."

"Does he?" Heavenly asked.

"He's very rich, you know," Samara said.

"Samara!" I said in a warning voice. "You're not supposed to say things like that."

"But it's true," Samara said.

"Of course it's true," Heavenly said with a wry smile. "Plenty of rich people teach piano."

Sometimes it was hard to tell when Heavenly was kidding. But I was pretty sure this was one of them.

"Well, maybe *he's* not rich," Samara admitted, "but his family is. Haven't you ever heard of Shackelford Semi-Conductors?"

"Let me guess," said Heavenly. "A semi-conductor is someone who conducts half an orchestra?"

"No!" Samara creased her forehead. "Semi-conductors do something in computers. Robby knows. Right?"

Robby nodded.

"Anyway, Dad said that the Shackelford family has tons of money because of their semi-conductors, so that makes Wes rich," said

Samara. Then, a little uncertainly, she turned to me. "Doesn't it, Kit?"

"I don't know," I answered.

"Well, if it's true, good for him," said Heavenly.

"If you married him, you wouldn't have to be a nanny anymore," Samara said.

"Why not?" asked Heavenly.

"Because you'd be rich, silly," Samara said as if it were obvious. "You could hire your own nanny."

"Maybe I like being a nanny," said Heavenly.

Samara made a face. "How could anyone *like* being a nanny?"

"How could anyone *like* teaching piano to little smarties who never practice?" Heavenly asked back.

The lock in the front door clicked. The door opened and Mom came in carrying a briefcase in one hand and a black leather bag filled with papers over her shoulder.

In a flash, Heavenly jumped up from the couch and headed for the door.

"Everyone's fed," she stated to Mom. "Tyler's had his bath and gone to bed. He seemed a little tired tonight. The children were supposed to clean the kitchen, but I haven't checked."

"We did," I said.

"See you." Heavenly picked up the brown over-the-shoulder bag and headed for the door.

"Wait," Mom said.

Heavenly stopped. "What?"

"What about the weekend?" Mom asked.

Heavenly scowled for a moment. "That's what parents are for," she said, then turned and vanished into the night.

Chapter

The next morning I woke up to a rude shock—the sound of vacuuming. It may have been Saturday morning but Fortuna was there, vacuuming and dusting and straightening. When I asked her why, she said that Mom had called her the night before and told her to come in first thing in the morning and fix up the house so that it would look nice when the new nannies came to be interviewed.

When I got down to the kitchen, Mom was already there, dressed in black jogging tights. Spread out on the kitchen table was her "Nanny File." Mom kept everything in neat files and this one listed every nanny agency and all her contacts and leads for finding nannies.

"Someone called," she said, while I looked around the kitchen for something to eat.

"Who?" I asked.

"A boy."

I stopped looking for something to eat. "What boy?"

Briiiinng! The phone rang. Mom answered and I listened to her make the same speech I'd heard her make a million times before.

What Mom Said	What She Really Meant
Our current nanny isn't working out	We hate her and/or she hates us
We're looking for someone who can start right away	We're desperate
We're willing to pay your plane fare	We're *really* desperate
References would help	We'll believe anything you tell us
Personality is the most important thing	We don't care if you can't cook or change a diaper. We need someone now!

Mom made an appointment for an interview and hung up.

"You said a boy called," I said.

"Right. It's here somewhere." Mom started to look through her papers. Then the phone rang again and she had to answer it.

I could see that this was going to take a while, so I figured I better get breakfast. The only thing I found was cold cereal—the same stuff all the old nannies had us eat. I can't say I really mind cold cereal (unless it's stale). What I minded was what cold cereal represented.

So why couldn't I make my own hot breakfast? After all, it was Saturday morning and it wasn't like there was someplace I had to be.

I decided to try something simple, like scrambled eggs and toast. I noticed Mom giving me a funny look as I cracked the eggs into a bowl and added some milk. I was mixing it all up when Robby and Samara came in.

"You're making breakfast?" Samara made a face.

"Could you make enough for me, too?" Robby asked eagerly.

"Sure." I cracked in two more eggs and added more milk.

"What's with you?" Samara asked.

"Why can't I make breakfast?" I asked back.

"You never did before," Samara said.

"Maybe I've changed," I said.

"How do you know what to do?" Robby asked.

"It's not brain surgery, Robby. I watched Heavenly."

"I hope you haven't grown attached to that person," Mom said as she hung up the phone. "Because I'm going to spend the weekend looking for a new nanny. And as soon as I find one, Miss Litebody is going to be ancient history."

"You're mad because of last night, right?" Robby asked.

"She was incredibly rude," Mom replied.

"But she was mad because she thought you were rude to her," I tried to explain.

"I think Mom's right," Samara said. "Heavenly definitely doesn't know her place. Making us do our homework at the kitchen table and clean up after meals. I mean, *really!*"

"I like her more than any other nanny we've ever had," I said. "I don't care if she's strict and makes us do chores. She's a good person and she really cares about us."

"If she cares so much about us, how come she left so fast last night?" Samara asked.

"Because Mom came home," I said. "I mean, can you really blame her? After being cooped up in the house all week with a bunch of crazy kids, wouldn't you want to get out too?"

"There's no point in discussing this anymore," Mom said as she picked up the phone and started to dial yet another nanny agency. "Heavenly is not coming back."

"But what about—?" I began.

"Oh, right," Mom said, and lifted up a piece of paper. "It was someone named Roy Chandler."

"Did he say what he wanted?" I asked.

"Something about being depressed?" Mom said absently as she went through other papers.

"It's a history project we're doing," I explained. "About the Great Depression."

Mom gave me a crooked smile. "I'm going to have a great depression if I don't find a new nanny by tomorrow night."

The phone rang again and Mom went into her nanny speech. Meanwhile, I wondered why Roy would call on a Saturday morning to talk about our history project. It wasn't due for a month and we'd already agreed on what each of us was going to do.

As soon as Mom got off the phone, I called Roy's house. His sister Dee Dee answered.

"You just missed him," she said. "That's too bad. He really wanted to talk to you."

"Do you know what it was about?" I asked.

Dee Dee said she didn't know. But Roy and his dad had gone to a conference for inventors and wouldn't be back until late the next night. That meant I would have to wait until school on Monday to find out why he'd called. It was disappointing, but there was nothing I could do about it.

For the rest of the day Mom interviewed a steady stream of nannies. They came in all sizes and shapes. Chunky blond ones with pretty faces. Skinny dark-haired ones with big hairdos. Old ones with wrinkled skin and bony fingers. Each time a new nanny arrived, Mom paraded us out for show-and-tell. Chance, of course, was nowhere to be found.

It was so dumb. Every time we were paraded out the nannies would smile and say things like "What cute kids" and "Such darlings."

I began to wish that just once one of them would say something like, "Look at those disgusting monsters!" or "I hate children! I must be crazy to want this job!" or "Yes, what delicious-looking little children. By the way, did any of my references mention that I'm a cannibal?"

But, of course, none of them said anything like that. And I know why. Over the past two years I'd made a study of nannies and what they liked and didn't like. Here's what I've learned:

What Nannies Like	What They Don't Like
Big houses so they can get away from everyone	Little houses where they can't get away

Parents who are gone most of the time and don't see what they do	Parents who are around most of the time and watch them
Families where most of the kids can dress and go potty by themselves	Families with lots of babies
Kitchens with big refrigerators	Little refrigerators

So I guess you could say that we offered pretty much the perfect situation for a nanny. I had no doubt Mom would find one before the weekend was over.

Chapter

22

On Sunday night Mom ordered in a big Chinese meal from the restaurant in town. Usually it was one of our favorite meals, but that night we kids ate silently while Mom and Dad went over all the nannies they'd interviewed during the weekend.

Mom and Dad ate with chopsticks while Chance, Robby and I used silverware. Tyler ate with his fingers and Samara tried to eat with chopsticks, but couldn't quite get it. No matter what she tried to pick up, it always fell off the chopstick before it got to her mouth.

"I don't understand how you eat with these," she complained.

"You want to know how you eat with chopsticks?" Chance asked.

Samara nodded.

"Easy," said Chance. "You leave them on the table beside your plate and eat with a knife and fork instead. *That's* how you eat with chopsticks."

Samara made a face. "You're so *not* funny, Chance."

"Why do you want to use them anyway?" Robby asked.

"Someday I might go to Japan," Samara replied.

"You don't think they have knives and forks in Japan?" I asked.

"That's not the point," Samara said in a huff. "If you want to be an international business traveler like Mom and Dad, you have to know how to get along in a lot of different places."

"It would help if you knew how to get along at home first," Chance chuckled.

Mom and Dad spread sheets of paper all over their part of the table and went over their nanny notes.

"What did you think of Bertha?" Mom asked Dad.

"You're thinking of hiring a nanny named *Bertha?*" Chance asked in disbelief.

"How about a nanny named Heavenly?" Robby asked.

"Absolutely not," answered Mom. She turned to Dad. "Bertha was one of the few who said she could start tomorrow morning. We could call her right now."

The rest of us finished our meals in silence. When we were done, we automatically started to clean up. Samara wiped the table. Chance swept the floor. Robby scraped the dishes and I loaded them into the dishwasher.

I noticed that Mom and Dad were staring at us.

"What's wrong?" I asked.

"Since when do the four of you clean up after dinner?" Mom asked.

"Heavenly taught us to do it," I said.

Mom and Dad traded looks.

"I guess having her around hasn't been a total loss," Dad said.

By the time I left the kitchen, Mom was on the phone, telling "Bertha" that she'd been hired and she should be at our house tomorrow morning at 7 A.M.

Out in the front hall, Dad and Robby were standing by the keypad for the alarm system.

"What's up?" I asked.

"I'm helping Dad enter the new code," Robby answered.

"New code?" I repeated.

"We always have a new code when we start a new nanny," Dad said. "Just to be safe." He turned to Robby. "Now, how do I do this again?"

I went into the living room and watched TV. I was really hoping Roy would get back from his conference early and call. But after a while I decided to go upstairs. As I went down the hall to my room, I noticed that Chance's bedroom door was open. Chance was sitting at his desk. Robby was sitting on Chance's bed. I don't think I'd ever seen Robby in Chance's bedroom before. I stopped in the doorway.

"What's up?"

"Robby told me Dad changed the code on the alarm," Chance said. "Guess it's New Nanny Time again."

"I guess."

"I'm gonna miss Heavenly," Robby said. The corners of his mouth turned down.

"Me, too," I said.

For a moment, we were all quiet. There didn't seem to be anything more to say.

Chapter

23

The next morning I was awakened by the sound of voices coming from downstairs. It was pretty early and I couldn't imagine what was going on, but now that I was up, I decided to go down and see.

I pulled on a robe and went out into the hall. Robby was already standing in the hall in his green Kermit pajamas. It was obvious that he was listening.

"What's going on?" I whispered.

"I'm not sure," Robby whispered back. "It's Dad and a couple of men, but I can't tell what they're talking about."

"Let's go see," I said.

We'd just started down the steps when I suddenly stopped and sniffed the air. "Wait a minute!"

"Smells like cooking!" Robby exclaimed. "You think it's Heavenly?"

"It can't be," I said. Just the same, I started down the steps twice as fast as before. Robby was right behind me.

We reached the bottom of the stairs. Dad was standing in the front hall with two men dressed in gray jumpsuits and matching baseball caps. One of them was tall and skinny and carried a flashlight. The other was short and fat and had a small black box with two red wires sticking out of it. Dad was dressed for work. He was wearing a perfectly pressed blue suit, a white shirt and red tie.

"I want to know how she got in," Dad said to the men in the jumpsuits.

The tall man with the flashlight scratched his neck. "I'm sorry, Mr. Rand, but she must've known the access code."

"That's impossible," Dad said. "We just changed it last night."

"It's not the alarm system, Mr. Rand," said the short man. "I've checked it out completely."

"You're saying it couldn't have been by-passed?" Dad asked.

"No, sir," both men answered at the same time.

"This is the state-of-the-art system," said the short man.

"Completely foolproof," said the man with the flashlight.

From the way Dad sighed and checked his wristwatch I knew he was late for an appointment.

"All right," he finally said. "Thanks for coming over."

"Sure thing, Mr. Rand," said the short man.

"Anytime," said the tall man.

Dad opened the front door for them. Parked in the driveway was a white van with ARTFUL ALARM SYSTEMS written on the side. Parked behind that was the black car that sometimes took Dad to work in the morning and brought him home at night. It wasn't exactly a chauffeured limousine, just a shiny black car driven by a man wearing a suit and tie.

Dad bent down to pick up his briefcase. As he did, he noticed Robby and me.

"Did one of you give Heavenly the new alarm code?" he asked.

Robby and I shook our heads.

"Well, someone must have, because she's in the kitchen cooking breakfast," Dad said.

Beep! Outside, the men in the van tapped their horn. They wanted to get going, but the black car was blocking them.

"I have to go," Dad said. "We'll talk about this tonight."

Dad went out the front door. Robby and I headed for the kitchen. Inside, Heavenly was cooking up breakfast.

"What are you doing here?" I cried.

"Cooking breakfast," she answered simply, but I thought I detected just the slightest hint of a smile.

"How'd you get in?" Robby asked.

"How do you want your eggs?" Heavenly asked back.

"Answer my question," Robby insisted.

"Say, 'Please answer my question,'" Heavenly corrected him.

"Okay, *please* answer my question," said Robby.

"What kind of toast?" Heavenly asked. "White, whole wheat or rye?"

"Hey! I thought you were going to answer my question," Robby complained.

"She's not going to tell you," I said and looked at Heavenly. "I'm really happy you're back. How was your weekend?"

"Okay," she said.

"Did you see your boyfriend?" Robby asked.

"None of your business," Heavenly replied.

"How on earth . . . ?" It was Mom. We all turned. She was wearing her robe and had a sleepy-looking Tyler in her arms. Tyler scowled at Heavenly, then rubbed his eyes with his pudgy little fists and blinked, as if over the weekend he'd forgotten who she was and was now slowly remembering.

"Horsey!" Reaching his arms out, he suddenly began to squirm out of Mom's grasp. "Horsey! Horsey!"

But Mom didn't want to let go of him.

"How did you get in?" Mom asked Heavenly.

"Horsey! Horsey!" Tyler kept reaching and squirming.

"Would you like me to give Tyler breakfast?" Heavenly asked.

"No, I'd like you to answer my question," Mom replied.

"She's not going to," I said.

Mom frowned. "What do you mean?"

"Horsey! Horsey!"

"We've been asking her things like that ever since she got here and she won't tell us," I said.

"Well, maybe she won't tell you, but she'd better tell me," Mom said.

"Why?" Robby asked.

"Horsey! Horsey!" Tyler was still kicking and squirming.

"Why?" Mom repeated. "Because . . ."

Her voice trailed off. I guess she'd just realized that as far as she was concerned, Heavenly didn't work for us anymore.

"Well, then, I think you'd better leave, Miss Litebody," Mom said.

"Who'll take care of Tyler?" I asked.

"Horsey!" Tyler had finally managed to squirm and twist out of Mom's arms. She had no choice but to lower him to the floor. He waddled across the floor and instantly glued himself to Heavenly's leg.

Mom glowered at Robby and me. "Are you *sure* one of you didn't let her in this morning?"

"I swear!" Robby cried.

"Me too." I raised my hand.

I don't think she believed us. But she was giving up. No doubt she was already starting to think about going to work. "All right, Miss Litebody, thank you very much for coming back and cooking breakfast. But as soon as Bertha arrives, I'm afraid your employment here will be over."

Mom turned and left the kitchen. As soon as she was gone, Heavenly turned and gave us a dour look. "Bertha?"

"Our new nanny," Robby explained. "I mean, *we* didn't want her. At least, me and Kit and Chance didn't."

"It's Kit and Chance and I," Heavenly corrected him.

"Whatever." Robby shrugged. "We really wanted you to stay. And if you count Tyler,

Todd Strasser

that's four against one. Even if you count our parents, it's still four against three. Which is a majority. And in most places a majority wins. Just not here."

That's when Samara and Chance came down.

"What are you doing here?" Samara asked when she saw Heavenly.

"She came back to cook us breakfast one last time," Robby said.

"Cool." Chance grinned.

"It's not cool," Samara said. "What about the new nanny?"

"You see a new nanny?" Robby asked. "I don't."

"You know she'll be here soon," Samara said. "Mom and Dad hired her last night."

"If I were you I'd chill out and enjoy the last hot breakfast you'll probably have for a long time," Chance advised.

Samara didn't argue. Instead, she got a plate like the rest of us and took her breakfast to the kitchen table.

Just before seven o'clock, Mom came back down to the kitchen in her work clothes. We were finishing breakfast. Heavenly took Tyler upstairs to clean him up and the rest of us straightened up the kitchen. Mom had a puzzled look on her face.

"What is it, Mom?" I asked.

"I . . . I just can't get over the change in you

four," she said. "Eating hearty breakfasts and cleaning up the kitchen."

"Guess you could say it's sort of *heavenly*, huh?" I winked.

Mom gave me a crooked smile. "You really like her, don't you?"

"Not me," Samara was quick to volunteer.

"Me and Kit and . . ." Robby began and then caught himself. "I mean, Kit and Chance and I like her."

"Well, I'm sorry." Mom looked up at the clock. "But it's too late. Bertha's due here any moment now."

"You could tell her you've changed your mind," I said hopefully.

"No," Mom said. "That wouldn't be fair. And besides, I still don't think I want Miss Litebody working for us."

It was just after seven o'clock when we finished straightening the kitchen and headed upstairs to get ready for school.

Twenty minutes later when I came back down to the first floor, Mom was sitting at the kitchen table with a cup of coffee. She was drumming her fingers on the tabletop.

"This is *not* a good sign," she mumbled to herself. She hated it when people weren't on time.

Robby came into the kitchen. "So where's Big Bertha?"

"Not here," I said.

"I don't understand it," Mom said. "She sounded very excited about the job on the phone last night. She said she'd be here at seven o'clock sharp. She knows how to get here because she came for the interview on Saturday."

"Maybe she got a better offer," Robby said.

"Between late last night and now?" Mom replied.

Chance and Samara came down next. Mom glanced at the clock again. It was getting close to the time when she should have been going to work and we should have been going to school.

Mom went to the phone and dialed a number. "Hello? This is Arlene Rand. Is Bertha there? Bertha Jones. You've never heard of her? Wait a minute." Mom checked her nanny file. "Is this 555-1879? Then she must be there. I called her at this number just last night. What? But I don't understand. I did too speak to her. That's not possible. *What?* Well, the same to *you!*"

Mom slammed down the phone. "The nerve of some people." She turned to the nanny file. "Let's see. I must have been mistaken. No, it's the right number." She closed the file. "I don't understand it."

It was getting late now. Mom glanced at her watch and then at the kitchen clock. You could almost read her mind. She had to go to work.

"What are we going to do?" Robby asked.

The words were hardly out of his mouth when Heavenly returned to the kitchen with Tyler in her arms. Tyler had the biggest smile on his face.

Mom pushed herself up from the kitchen table. "I can't wait any longer. I have to get to work. Is there any chance, Miss Litebody, that you could stay a day or two longer? Just until I can get this situation straightened out?"

The question floated in the air like the aroma of Heavenly's delicious breakfast. Suddenly I realized that there was no reason why she had to say yes. After all, Mom and Dad weren't treating her very nicely. Wouldn't this be the perfect revenge?

Heavenly silently considered Mom's question. I think Mom was just realizing that the answer she wanted was not guaranteed.

"We'll pay you for your time, of course," Mom hastily added.

Heavenly hardly reacted. It almost seemed as if she didn't care a hoot about the money. She glanced at Chance, Robby and me. We all nodded eagerly, as if to say, "Please stay, please!"

Then she turned to Mom. "All right," she said. "But I'll warn you again. Once I'm gone, I'll never come back."

Mom's mouth fell open. She looked so surprised. For a moment I thought she was going to say something. But then she just nodded and hurried out of the kitchen.

Chapter

It was time to go to school. Once again my thoughts turned to Roy. We all gathered at the front door and waited while Robby punched the code in the alarm system keypad.

Suddenly a small red light on the keypad started to blink on and off.

"Darn it!" Robby grumbled and tried entering the code again.

"What's wrong?" Heavenly asked.

"It's the code," Robby said. "Dad and I entered a new one last night, but the alarm isn't recognizing it."

"Or maybe you just forgot it," Samara said.

Robby glowered at her.

"Being mean doesn't help," Heavenly scolded.

Samara made a face but didn't say anything.

Meanwhile, Robby tried the code again, but the red light kept flashing.

"Let's just go," Chance said impatiently.

"You'll set off the alarm," I warned him. "And we'll have to pay a fine." Most of the security systems in our neighborhood were connected to the police station. If the police came and it was a false alarm, they gave you a ticket.

"What this family needs is a dog," Heavenly said.

"Wait a minute," Robby said. "You got in this morning, so you must know the code."

"That's right," I said. "Not that you'll ever tell us how you knew it."

Everyone looked at Heavenly.

"Robby," she said. "I suggest you take a deep breath and try again."

"What's the point?" Robby argued. "I've done it three times already and it hasn't worked."

"Just do it," Heavenly said.

"It's dumb," Robby replied.

Instead of arguing with him, Heavenly leveled her gaze at me. She touched her left ear. It was the strangest thing. I felt an odd, slightly dizzy sensation. Sort of the way you feel after spinning around in a circle a few times. Was I imagining it? Or was it something Heavenly was doing?

"Try it again, Robby," I heard myself say. "I bet this time it'll work."

"Here's goes nothing." Robby pressed the keypad again.

The red light stopped flashing and the green light went on.

"What the . . ." Robby frowned.

"We better get going." Heavenly started to push Tyler's stroller. "We don't want to be late, do we?"

We left the house and started toward school. Chance jogged off to be with his friends. I still couldn't figure out what had happened between Heavenly and me. I decided I'd ask her about it just as soon as we were alone.

I hardly noticed when a car passed and then stopped ahead of us.

"Kit?" Jessica Huffington got out of the car. "I have to talk to you."

The next thing I knew, Heavenly went ahead, pushing the stroller, with Robby and Samara. Meanwhile, Jessica and I fell behind and walked together.

"Roy called me last night," Jessica said in a low voice as we walked. Almost instantly I felt jealous. Why had Roy called *her* and not *me*?

"To talk about our project?" I guessed.

"Well, that's what it seemed like," Jessica said. "But you know how sometimes someone calls for one reason but after a while you get the feeling it's really about something else?"

I felt like groaning. If Jessica told me that she thought Roy liked her . . .

"Anyway, we talked about the project for a while," Jessica went on, "and then it was like there was nothing else to talk about and I was beginning to think he was just going to say good-bye and hang up. And guess what?"

"What?"

"He asked if you ever said anything about him."

Why is she telling me this? I wondered. *Has it ever occurred to her that she's not the only . . .*

"Kit?" Jessica interrupted my thoughts.

"Yes?"

"Did you hear what I just said?"

"Sure, you said that Roy was just about to hang up when he asked . . ."

"If *you* ever said anything about him," Jessica finished the sentence for me.

"Me?" I said, stunned.

"Yes, *you!*"

"Why?"

"Why do you think?" Jessica asked with a grin. "Because he *likes* you!"

Can you blame me if I spent the rest of our walk in a fog? I'm not sure which was more shocking—that Roy had let Jessica know that he liked me, or that Jessica had gone out of her way to tell me.

Jessica and I got to school and started down the hall.

"Kit?" Someone called my name.

I turned. Roy Chandler was coming out of a room, holding some flowers. At first I thought it looked cute. Then I realized he was bringing the flowers *to me!*

Right in the middle of the hall!

With everyone watching!

My face began to glow like a red-hot ember.

"I picked these for you, Kit," Roy said, holding out the flowers.

"How romantic!" Jessica clasped her hands and gushed.

By now a crowd had formed. Some kids were giggling. Others were snickering. I didn't know what to do.

"Go on, Kit," someone said. "Take the flowers or you'll hurt Romeo Roy's feelings!"

Everyone laughed. I know I should have appreciated what Roy was doing, but all I felt was total embarrassment. Meanwhile, Roy had the goofiest look on his face. Almost as if he was under a spell.

I took the flowers from him. Everyone cheered. Then they began to chant like a bunch of immature second graders:

Todd Strasser

Kit and Roy, sitting in a tree
K-I-S-S-I-N-G.
First comes love, then comes marriage.
Then comes babies in the baby carriage!
Kiss, kiss, we want a kiss!

No way! I thought. Then I looked at Roy.
He was moving closer.
And starting to pucker his lips.

Chapter

"He wanted to kiss you *in the middle of the hall?*" Darcy gasped at lunch. We weren't sitting at our regular table. We were sitting at the far end of the cafeteria.

"Uh-huh."

"That's weird," she said.

"Oh, yeah."

"What did you do?" she asked.

"I shook his hand, then turned around and got out of there as fast as I could." I was sitting with my back to the rest of the cafeteria.

"Why are we sitting here?" Darcy asked.

"I'm hiding," I said.

"From who?"

"Everyone. But especially Roy. Do you see him?"

Darcy, who was sitting across from me, and

therefore was facing the whole cafeteria, looked over my shoulder. "Yes, I do."

"What's he doing?" I asked.

"Staring at you."

"Oh, no."

"Well." Darcy smiled. "You always said you wanted him to like you."

"Yes, but not *this much*," I replied. "I mean, this is embarrassing. He's acting totally weird."

"Talk about weird," Darcy said. "I finally remembered to ask my mom about your nanny's name. Remember I told you it sounded familiar?"

"Uh-huh."

"Well, guess what?" she said. "It turns out that the Litebodys were the original settlers of Soundview Manor. Not only that, but somewhere around the early 1930s the family vanished mysteriously. No one ever knew what happened to them."

"That was around the time of the Great Depression," I said.

"Maybe they just got really depressed," Darcy joked.

But to me, it just made everything about Heavenly a little more mysterious. Tabs breaking off soda cans, doorknobs falling off doors, brand new backpacks ripping, getting through the alarm system, boys suddenly falling totally in love. And I was still almost certain the door to my room had been locked the night Heavenly came in. What was going on?

After school I waited for Robby and Samara and we all walked home together.

"So how long do you think Heavenly will stay?" Robby asked.

"Who knows?" I answered. "Until Mom and Dad hire a new nanny, I guess."

"Don't you think it's kind of strange?" Robby asked. "I mean, the way that Bertha nanny didn't show up this morning? Mom was positive she was going to be there."

"Why do you care?" Samara asked. "She's just a nanny. They're all just nannies. They don't care about us. All they care about is getting paid and going out on the weekends and meeting boys."

"I think Heavenly cares," Robby said.

"Because she cooks?" Samara asked. "Maybe she just likes to cook. One thing I don't like is how she bosses us around."

"She only does it because she knows what's right for us," I said.

"Oh, really?" Samara snorted. "And who made her so high and mighty?"

We got home and let ourselves into the house. Almost instantly I heard laughter and squeals coming from the kitchen. I don't know why, but they didn't sound like the usual laughter and squeals.

I went into the kitchen. Robby and Samara followed. Heavenly was sitting on the floor with her back toward me. Tyler was on his hands and knees. He seemed to be reaching for something, but Heavenly's back was blocking my view and I couldn't tell what it was.

"Gently now, Tyler," Heavenly was saying. "It's not a doll. It's a real live thing."

What!? Sensing something truly amazing, I quickly stepped around Heavenly. There on the floor was the cutest, pudgiest, most adorable little tan puppy I'd ever seen!

Chapter

"Puppy! Puppy!" Tyler squealed happily when he saw me.

"Whose is it?" I asked, shocked.

"Ours," Heavenly answered. "And it's a *he*."

"Ours?" repeated Robby, amazed.

"Yours, mine, Tyler's, Kit's, Samara's, everyone's," Heavenly said.

"You got us a dog?" I couldn't believe it.

"Wait till Mom and Dad see this," Samara smirked.

Even though Robby and I really wanted to play with the new puppy, Heavenly made us do our homework first. It wasn't so hard, really. Heavenly and Tyler must have played with the puppy for a long time before we got home because as soon as they stopped, he curled up into a little tan ball and went to sleep.

As soon as five o'clock came around and "free time" began, Robby and I woke the puppy up and started to play with him.

He really was the cutest little thing I'd ever seen, all pudgy and clumsy and playful.

"Does he have a name?" I asked.

"Not yet," answered Heavenly from the stove where she was cooking dinner. "By the way, Roy called before. I told him you were busy with your homework and that you'd call back later. I hope you're not mad."

I shook my head. I'd had a lot of Roy already that day. More than I ever dreamed about!

"Ow!" Robby suddenly yanked his finger away from the puppy's mouth. "He bit me!"

"No, silly, he's just playing," said Heavenly. "But you have to be careful of those sharp little baby teeth."

"You're telling me," Robby grumbled.

"What kind is he?" I asked.

"Golden retriever," Heavenly said.

"Will he grow big?" Robby asked.

"Oh, yes," Heavenly said. "Eighty or ninety pounds, at least."

Eighty or 90 pounds! Robby and I stared at each other in wonder. That was bigger than Robby and almost as big as me.

"Are they good watchdogs?" I asked.

"Pretty good," said Heavenly. "Until they get to know you. Then they're just big pussycats."

"Talk about cats," Samara said. "What does Puff think of him?"

"Haven't seen much of Puff today," Heavenly said.

"So what else is new?" said Robby. "I never see that cat."

"That's because Tyler put her in the dryer," Samara said.

I was curious about something. "How do you know so much about dogs, Heavenly?"

"Oh, I've had lots of them," she answered.

"Really? Where? When?"

Heavenly suddenly looked up from the stove. She knew what I was doing, and I think she also knew that I almost got away with it.

"Wouldn't you like to know?" she said with a smile.

"Where'd you get him?" Robby asked.

"From someone I know," Heavenly answered mysteriously.

Chance came home just before dinnertime.

"Whoa! Cool!" he grinned broadly when he saw the puppy. "What's his name?"

"He doesn't have one," I said.

"Then let's make one up," Chance said.

"Maybe we shouldn't," said Robby. "I hate to

say this, but before we give him a name, I think we better see what Mom and Dad say."

Everyone got quiet for a moment.

"He's right," I said, feeling a little glum. "What's the point of giving him a name when Mom and Dad probably won't let us keep him?"

"Probably?" Samara gave a nasty chuckle. "You mean *definitely.*"

Dinner that night was pretty gloomy. Robby and I picked at our food, but neither of us was really hungry. Even Tyler was quiet, as if he sensed something wasn't right.

"Wow, I didn't expect this," said Heavenly as she ate. "I thought you'd all be thrilled."

"We are thrilled," I said. "That's the problem. Robby and Samara are right. As soon as Mom and Dad get home, they're going to go nuclear."

"Oh, I don't know," Heavenly said. "I've seen their type before. I bet their bark is a lot worse than their bite." She nodded over at the puppy, who was sleeping on an old blanket in a cardboard box. "You really think they'll be able to resist that adorable little creature?"

"Oh, yeah," Robby said with a nod. "You better believe they'll be able to resist it."

"I don't know where you got that puppy from," said Samara, "but if I were you I'd call them up right now and make sure they'll take him back."

"You're such a bunch of pessimists," Heavenly said. "I think you're going to be in for a big surprise."

I hoped she was right, but deep in my heart, I had serious doubts.

Chapter

27

Mom rarely got home from work before seven-thirty and Dad usually didn't walk in the door until nine. After dinner, I went up to my room to type an essay on my computer. I heard a phone ring and then Heavenly's voice came over the intercom: *"Kit, it's Roy."*

I went out to the hall and called back to Heavenly to tell Roy I was taking a shower. It wasn't that I didn't like him anymore, it was just that I wasn't sure what to *do* with him. And to be honest, after that scene with the flowers in the hall at school that day, I was nervous about what he'd try next.

I stood in the hall for a moment. I could hear music coming from Chance's room, and muffled cries and explosions coming from Robby's room, where he was no doubt playing video games.

If I really concentrated, I could hear faint laughter and splashing coming from the bathroom in the other wing where Heavenly was giving Tyler his nightly bath. I couldn't remember Tyler sounding so happy.

It was nearly nine when I heard the front door open and close. Usually, if it was this late, it meant Mom and Dad had come home together.

I left my room. When I got out into the hall, Robby and Chance were already there, heading down the stairs. I hurried after them.

"What in the world?" Mom's voice rang up from the kitchen.

"Where did this come from?" I heard Dad ask.

A moment later I joined everyone in the kitchen. Mom and Dad were staring down into the cardboard box. Inside, the puppy was yipping and wagging his tail as if he wanted to play. He pressed his little front paws against the side of the box and scratched at it as if trying to climb out.

The kitchen door swung open and Samara came in.

Mom looked up. "I'm all ears, kids."

"Heavenly got him," Samara reported.

Mom and Dad shared a grim look. As if they weren't surprised.

"Where is she?" Dad asked.

"Up in her room, I guess," I said.

"I think this is really it," Mom said.

Dad nodded. "All right. I want all of you to go back to your rooms and stay there until I tell you that you can come out."

He left the kitchen.

"Why'd he say that?" Robby asked.

"It's obvious," Samara said. "This time he's going to kick Heavenly out for good."

Robby and I started out of the kitchen.

"Don't go," Mom said.

"But—" I began.

"I'm sorry, kids, but this will never work out," Mom said firmly. "She has to go."

"But it's not her fault," I said.

"We like her," said Robby. "She's the best nanny we've ever had."

"I know you think that," Mom replied. "But it's too late."

"Why?" I asked.

"Because Miss Litebody doesn't understand that nannies are not supposed to do certain things," Mom calmly explained. "Nannies do not bring dogs into the house. They do not act as if they *own* the house. They do not make the rules. The problem with Miss Litebody is that she does whatever she pleases. And in this family that can't possibly work. Now I want you to do what your father said and go to your rooms."

I spent the rest of the night in my room and

only went out to wash up. I hoped to run into Robby or Chance in the hall, but I didn't, so I just went to bed and turned out the lights.

Sometimes at night just as I fell asleep I'd pretend I was shipwrecked on a sandy island with palm trees and beautiful clear blue water all around. A small boat would appear on the horizon, sailing toward me. Sometimes it was a sailboat, sometimes a motorboat, sometimes one of those rubber boats with a small outboard engine.

As the boat got closer I would stand knee-deep in the warm water and watch eagerly to see who was in it. Chance usually came in the motorboat. Roy Chandler came in the rubber boat. If it was the sailboat, it might be all sorts of people: our piano teacher, Wes; or Darcy; or sometimes someone I'd seen but didn't know.

That night as I stood in the water I watched a rowboat appear and come toward the island. As it came closer I could see that it was being rowed by someone with purple hair. The sunlight glinted off the hoops in her ears and I could see tattoos on her bare arms.

She came closer. Now I could see a little puppy perched in the bow of the boat. His mouth was open and his tongue was hanging out and he was wagging his tail. His mouth moved and I expected to hear a cute little puppy bark.

But instead of a bark, the sound I heard was sad. Like a soft cry or a whimper.

It didn't make sense. The puppy in the bow of the rowboat looked happy.

But the sound he was making was so sad . . .

That's when I opened my eyes. I was lying in my bed. The room was dark. The island, the clear blue water and the rowboat were gone, but the sad little whimpers were still there.

The puppy! His first night in a new house and he was downstairs in the kitchen all alone in that cardboard box. No wonder he was crying.

I turned on the light and pulled on my robe. As I crossed my room toward the door, I heard another door creak. Someone else was coming out of their room. I expected to find Chance, or even Robby, who usually slept like a log, out in the hallway.

But it was Samara. She was standing in the doorway of her room with a puzzled expression on her face.

"What's that sound?" she whispered.

"The puppy," I answered in a low voice.

My half-sister's mouth fell open with surprise. "Really?"

"Why do you care?" I asked. "I thought you hated dogs."

Samara raised her chin. "I do . . . it's just that he sounds so sad."

"You'd be sad too if you were left alone all night in a strange place," I whispered.

Now I could hear low voices coming from the other wing.

"It's Mom and Dad," Samara whispered. "The puppy woke them, too."

"Oh, no," I whispered back. "Now they're *really* going to be mad."

Already I could hear two sets of footsteps on the stairs going down to the first floor.

I quickly headed down the hall. I wasn't sure what Mom and Dad would do. Suddenly I realized Samara was following me. I stopped and turned to her. "Where are you going?"

"Down to the kitchen," Samara answered.

"Why?" I asked.

Samara stuck her nose in the air. "I don't have to tell you."

When we got down to the kitchen, Mom and Dad were both there in their robes. They were staring down into the cardboard box as if they didn't know what to do.

I looked into the box. The puppy was on his hind legs again, scratching his little front paws against the side of the box as if he wanted to get out. He was whimpering and crying and looking up at us with those sweet, sad puppy dog eyes.

"Come here, little guy." I reached down and picked him up. As soon as he was cradled safely in my arms he stopped whimpering and started to lick my chin.

I couldn't believe the looks on Mom's, Dad's and Samara's faces.

"Aw, that's so cute," Samara cooed.

"I never saw a puppy like this before." Dad reached over and petted him gently on the head.

"Such an adorable little thing," added Mom.

Am I dreaming? I wondered.

"Uh, could we pause for a reality check here?" I said. "Is it my imagination or have all three of you gone mushy over this puppy?"

"I never said I didn't think puppies were cute," Mom insisted.

"Neither did I," said Samara.

"Let's just say I didn't know how cute they could be," added Dad, who was still petting the puppy on his fuzzy little head.

I started to kneel down.

"What are you doing?" Mom asked.

"Putting him down," I said. "Maybe if we let him run around a little, he'll get tired and go to sleep."

If you think how my parents and Samara reacted to the puppy was amazing, you won't believe what happened next. All four of us sat down on the kitchen floor and made a circle so that the puppy could run around between us. The funniest thing was putting him in our laps or on our legs and watching him fumble and tumble as he tried to climb off.

The kitchen was filled with laughter. I'd never seen Mom and Dad and Samara have so much fun.

"Here, let me have him," Dad would say.

"No, he's mine!" Samara would try to hold him.

"You have to share, Samara," Mom said.

"If you guys don't put him down and let him run around he'll never get tired," I complained.

"Oh, don't be such a stick in the mud," Mom scolded me as she hugged the puppy. "We're having fun."

"Uh, am I seeing things?" It was Chance, rubbing his eyes and standing in the kitchen doorway.

"Don't you start," Mom warned from her seat on the floor. "We just went through all this with Kit."

"Yeah," agreed Dad. "If you want to play with the puppy, get down on the floor with the rest of us. But if you're going to stand there and make cracks, you can go back to bed."

"Floor sounds good to me," Chance said and sat down.

It was late and everyone should have been in bed. Instead, we were sitting on the floor playing with a puppy. I couldn't remember the last

Todd Strasser

time a bunch of us just sat around and did something silly and meaningless and fun. I wanted to point that out, but I was afraid if I said it out loud I'd break the spell.

After another few minutes of playing with the puppy, Samara suddenly scooped him up in her arms and asked, "Can't we keep him?"

If anything should have broken the spell, it was that. For a moment, Mom and Dad both reacted with wide eyes, as if they'd just been awakened from a dream. They gave each other questioning looks.

"What do you think?" Mom asked Dad.

"Maybe we should try it for two weeks and see what happens," Dad said.

"Is that a yes?" Samara asked eagerly.

"I think it's a yes," said Chance.

"Me too," I agreed.

"Not so fast," Mom said. "We need some rules here. One, he stays in the kitchen at all times."

"But then he'll cry," Samara argued.

Mom sighed. "Okay, he stays in the kitchen during the day. At night one of you can take him up to your room."

"I'm first!" Samara blurted.

Chance reached over and put his hand on his sister's forehead. "Are you running a fever or something?"

"Drop dead," Samara snapped.

"Sounds to me like she's feeling fine," I said with a wink.

"Rule number two," said Mom. "You kids are totally in charge of feeding and taking care of him. And cleaning up any messes he makes."

We nodded and waited for rule number three.

Mom frowned. "I know there should be a rule number three, but I can't think of it right now."

"We'll give you a rain check," I said.

Dad looked up at the kitchen clock. "It's pretty late," he said. "We better get to bed."

Everyone started to get up, including Samara, who still had the puppy in her arms.

"There's just one thing," I said. "You guys fired Heavenly tonight because she got us this puppy."

Dad's shoulders sagged and Mom pursed her lips. They looked at each other.

"I hate to say it, but Kit's right," Dad said.

"It's almost as if she knew us better than we knew ourselves," Mom said.

"Can't you get her back?" Chance asked.

Dad raised his hands in a helpless gesture. "I wouldn't know where to begin. She's gone."

"We never even got a phone number from her," added Mom.

Chapter

So Heavenly was gone, but the puppy would stay. Back in bed, waiting to fall asleep, I felt sad but thankful. Even though she hadn't been with us for very long, I knew Heavenly had changed us all a little bit. Robby seemed a little more grown up. Chance seemed a little less wild. Mom, Dad and Samara all seemed to have realized that it was okay to be wrong about something.

As for me, I just felt a little better about everything. After all, Roy Chandler was now crazy about me, and we'd gotten a brand-new puppy (I wasn't sure *which* I was more excited about).

I was a bit worried that now that Heavenly was gone everyone might go back to the way they used to be. But then I thought maybe that was why Heavenly got us the puppy. Even without Heavenly, the puppy would remind us of how to be.

I can't swear, but I think I fell asleep that night with a smile on my face.

Chapter

29

Don't tell me that!" Dad's voice rumbled up the stairs the next morning and woke me.

"Gee, Mr. Rand, I'm really sorry."

"Sorry?" Dad repeated.

What in the world? I quickly pulled on my robe and went out into the hall. Robby, Chance and Samara were coming out of their rooms.

"I would really like an explanation!" Dad demanded. He sounded like he was trying to be serious but having a hard time. "I am absolutely sure I changed the code again. Now you tell me how this happened."

"What's going on?" Samara asked.

"I'm not sure," I said as I headed for the stairs, "but I've got my fingers crossed."

We'd just started down the steps when Chance said, "Smell that?"

"Smells like cooking!" I cried.

We raced down the stairs as fast as we could. Once again Dad was standing in the front hall with those two men from the alarm company. Our new puppy had grabbed the tall man's pants cuff with his mouth. He was tugging on the cuff and making cute little growling noises.

"I'm telling you, Mr. Rand," said the tall one, "she must've known the access code."

"No one knew the access code," Dad shot back. "I just made it up last night and I know I didn't tell anyone."

"All I can tell you is it's not the system, Mr. Rand," said the short man with the box. "I've checked it out completely. And this alarm system is the—"

"Yes, I know," Dad cut him short. "It's the state of the art."

Both men nodded.

"Completely foolproof," Dad said.

Both men nodded again.

Dad let out a big sigh. "Thanks for coming over."

"Sure thing, Mr. Rand," said the short man.

"Anytime," said the tall man. He tried to shake his leg gently, but our puppy refused to let go. Chance bent down and picked him up.

Dad opened the front door for them and they went out. Dad closed the door and shook his head. "State-of-the-art nonsense," he muttered.

"Hey, don't worry about it," Chance said, patting the puppy's head. "Pretty soon we'll have a state-of-the-art watchdog."

Meanwhile, I went into the kitchen. The table was set for breakfast, and Heavenly was behind the stove, cooking.

"You changed your mind!" I hurried around the counter and hugged her.

Heavenly gave me a puzzled look. "What are you talking about?"

"You said that once you'd gone you'd never come back," I said.

"Well, I'm here, aren't I?" she said.

"Yes, but—"

"If I'm here, I can't be gone," she said. "Now get your plate and have some breakfast."

"Yes, ma'am!" I grabbed a plate.

It wasn't long before the whole family was sitting at the kitchen table, eating Heavenly's breakfast. Heavenly sat with us and fed Tyler.

"Wow, I can't remember the last time we all ate breakfast together," I said.

"Especially on a weekday," added Chance.

"And I can't remember the last time we had a dog," said Robby.

"Maybe that's because we've never had one before," Samara groaned.

"Puppy! Puppy!" Tyler stretched out his arms

toward the puppy, who was chewing on an old dishrag.

"Not until you finish breakfast, Mr. Wiggler," Heavenly said.

"So Mom, Dad, is there anything you want to say to Heavenly?" I asked.

Mom and Dad gave each other questioning looks.

"I guess there is," Dad said.

Mom cleared her throat. "Miss Litebody, would you be willing to accept employment with our family as Tyler's nanny?"

Heavenly smiled. "Are you sure you want someone like me?"

"No," Mom said. "But we don't seem to have a choice."

Everyone had to laugh. It looked like Heavenly was here to stay. At least, for now.

About the Author

TODD STRASSER has written many award-winning novels for young and teenage readers. Among his best-known books are those in the Help! I'm Trapped In series and *How I Created My Perfect Prom Date*, which was made into the movie *Next to You* starring Melissa Joan Hart. He has also written *Shark Bite*, *Grizzly Attack*, *Buzzard's Feast*, and *Gator Prey* in the Against the Odds series, published by Minstrel Books. Todd speaks frequently at schools about the craft of writing and conducts writing workshops for young people. He and his wife, children, and Labrador retriever live in a suburb of New York City. Todd and his family enjoy boating, hiking and mountain climbing.

Log on to www.toddstrasser.com to learn more about Todd and the Here Comes Heavenly series.

Todd Strasser's

Here Comes Heavenly

Here Comes Heavenly

She just appeared out of nowhere. Spiky purple hair, tons of
earrings and rings. Hoops through her eyebrow and nostril,
and tattoos on both arms. She said her name was Heavenly
Litebody. Our Nanny. Nanny???

Dance Magic

Heavenly is cool and punk. She sure isn't the nanny our
parents wanted for my baby brother, Tyler. And what's with
all these ladybugs?

Pastabilities

Heavenly Litebody goes to Italy with the family and causes all
kinds of merriment! But...is the land of amore ready for her?

Spell Danger

Kit has to find a way to keep Heavenly Litebody, the Rand's
magical, mysterious nanny from leaving the family
forever.

**I'm 16,
I'm a witch,
and I still have
to go to school?**

**Look for a new title
every month
Based on the hit TV series**

READ THE
FINNEGAN ZWAKE

MYSTERIES BY MICHAEL DAHL

THE HORIZONTAL MAN

Thirteen-year-old Finnegan Zwake is staying with his Uncle Stoppard and life is fairly normal—until the day Finn discovers a dead body in the basement. It's in the storage area where Finn's parents left behind gold treasure from their last archaeological expedition. And missing from the storage space is a magnificent Mayan gold figure, the Horiztonal Man....

THE WORM TUNNEL

Finnegan is off to an archeological dig in sunny Agualar, land of the giant cacti, jungles, and dinosaurs. Dead ones, that is. While Finn and his uncle are searching for treasure, the crew is digging up very valuable dinosaur eggs. But digging too deeply can stir up trouble, not to mention a murder, or two, or three....

THE RUBY RAVEN

Finnegan's uncle is invited to be a finalist in an international mystery writer's award competition. That means exotic Saharan travel for Finn and Uncle Stoppard. The winner will receive $1,000,000 and The Ruby Raven, a figurine of a dark, carved bird, with the real ruby gems as eyes. All of the writers are eager to win this coveted award, in fact some are *dying* to possess it....

It's TV—in a book!
Don't miss a single hilarious episode of—

Don't Touch that Remote!

Episode 1: Sitcom School
Spencer's got his own TV show!
Watch him try to keep his wacky costars out of trouble!

Episode 2: The Fake Teacher
Is that new teacher all he seems?
And is Jay hiding something really, really big?

Episode 3: Stinky Business
Danny's got a brand-new career, and something smells!
Here's a clue: It ain't fish!

Episode 4: Freak Week
It's the spookiest show ever as the gang spends overnight
in their school.... Will Pam's next laugh be her last?

Tune in as Spencer, Pam, Danny, and Jay negotiate
the riotous world of school TV. Laugh out loud at
their screwball plots and rapid-fire TV-style joking.
Join in the one-liners as this over-the-top, off-the-wall,
hilarious romp leaves you screaming—
Don't Touch That Remote!

No mission is ever impossible!

Join the

on all of their supercool missions
as they jet-set around the world
in search of truth and justice!

The secret is out! Read

LICENSE TO THRILL
LIVE AND LET SPY
NOBODY DOES IT BETTER
SPY GIRLS ARE FOREVER
DIAL "V" FOR VENGEANCE
IF LOOKS COULD KILL